WHAT SHE DIDN'T KNOW
Book 2

Of Widowhood and Murder

Patricia E. Gitt

Print Edition ISBN 978-1-7345478-1-8

Ebook edition ISBN 978-1-7345478-2-5

This book was printed in the United States

What She Didn't Know, Book 1 – Blinded by love

Print Edition ISBN 1-7341584-9-6

Ebook Edition ISBN 1-7345478-0-1

Published by Athena Book Publishing

New York, New York

Athenabookpublishing.com

Also by Patricia E. Gitt

New York City Mysteries

CEO

ASAP – as soon as possible – A Settling of Scores

TBD – to be determined – A Game Changer

FYI – An Unintended Consequence

Website: patriciagitt.com

Dedication

This book is dedicated to MG Karpin, author and friend, for her patience and encouragement throughout this creative journey.

Quotation.

"Life shrinks or expands in proportion to one's courage."
~ Anais Nin

Contents

Prologue

What She Didn't Know – Book 1

Sally Compton was a lively and dedicated young executive assistant to Tyler Scott, who fell blindly in love with her boss. They marry. Readers follow the impassioned couple through early trials involving Tyler's first wife, the vicious Victoria, who makes it difficult for him to see his two children.

To show his love, Tyler books a trip of a lifetime to Antarctica in celebration of their fifth wedding anniversary. A trip that puts his already stretched budget into arrears. But anything to show Sally how much he loves her.

Unfortunately, Tyler dies and Sally begins to discover the many secrets Tyler has kept from her. At first embittered, she begins to gather information with which to deal with her husband's unexpected duplicity and vows to rebuild her life, one completely under her control.

Chapter 1

Stiff from sleeping in a cramped position, Sally rushed out of her apartment and with hands pressed against the hall wall just outside her door, she began stretching her calf muscles. When the elevator located three apartments away opened, she couldn't move fast enough before the door snapped close.

Shaking her head, she thought she'd seen an aberration. Something on the floor… a pile of fabric? The building kept the elevators and hallways clean with nary a spot, dent, or stain to mar the buildings' public spaces. Confused, she hurriedly pushed the down button once again. Thankfully, another elevator arrived in seconds, and sprinting in, she hit the button for the lobby. Without her morning coffee, she was still a bit foggy-minded… *Better watch my footing this morning or I'll trip and that would really mess up my day.*

"Hi, Joe," Sally greeted the building's doorman. He always had a smile for her at this early hour. One of the more pleasant things about her decision to move into the city and not stay isolated out in the suburbs. That was three years ago, 2018. Where did the time go?

"Joe, did you happen to see anything strange in the number 3 elevator?"

"No, Mrs. Scott. Let me check the camera. What do you think you saw?"

"This may sound crazy, but either someone dropped their coat or was slumped on the floor?"

"I do see something. I'll get it checked out. Enjoy your run."

Nodding, and with a wave, Sally walked out of the building's entrance and began a slow jog toward Broadway. At 6 a.m., the August morning sun had just begun to rise behind her. *Okay ole girl, down to 14th Street and back up via Irving Place, twice around Gramercy Park and home.* With the route set, she let her mind wander. It was a three-day-a-week ritual, rain or shine, and Sally, who only started to jog around the neighborhood after she signed her third client, now looked forward to the regularity of the exercise that let her mind roam free of problems and feelings of loneliness.

What was in the elevator? she wondered as she continued her leisurely pace. *Joe will find out. He's a font of building information.* She'd just rounded Broadway and headed south when her mind turned to business. *Need to update my website. The language is a bit wonky. It needs a friendlier touch. While presenting my accounting services, the site has to show my personal connection with clients. Check the calendar for second quarter tax filings. I think I have everyone's papers, but Freddie's. Okay, a Zoom session to get him in gear. Shit. I'd rather stop by his beauty salon and pick up his papers. He usually forgets some little item. This COVID shutdown is beginning to get on my nerves. I can visit all my clients but Freddie. He insists that for the present, unless absolutely necessary, conversations can be done online. What is he afraid of? I'm fully vaccinated and work from home. Who am I going to infect?*

By the time she had returned to the building, she had her morning's tasks lined up. Entering the lobby, she approached the doorman's station, panting from having picked up her normal pace on the last leg of her run. Sally hoped Joe found nothing unusual. Maybe someone simply dropped their coat on the elevator floor. "Joe?"

"Mrs. Scott, just a moment, please," Joe said and returned to his conversation on the building's house phone.

Curiosity had her study the young man's face for clues. Normally friendly, she had seen him during difficult situations with an anxious tenant or angry delivery man, and yet he remained diplomatically unruffled.

"Mrs. Scott, I called the police and they are in the basement going over the elevator now."

"Police? Maybe I was just having one of my caffeine-deprived moments?"

"I'm sorry I don't have any information as yet. And you know the building rules… not to talk about incidents or building residents," Joe replied apologetically as he gave a quick look over his shoulder.

"But the police? It's not like we live in a crime-ridden building."

"I am sorry," Joe replied. And looking up behind his doorman's station, Sally saw the camera installed by the building's managing agent to keep tabs on the staff. *Funny, I never noticed that before*. Nodding her understanding of his situation, she waved and headed toward the elevators and home for a shower. For some reason, even with a relatively cool morning, she was drenched in perspiration.

Chapter 2

The air was hot and stuffy in the sub-basement of the apartment building with the medical examiner, her assistant, and detective, Jace Logan, crowded around the open elevator. Detective Logan had finished speaking to the uniformed patrolman a few minutes earlier. He had been first on the scene. But his information had been limited to his checking to see if the woman was dead, and calling the precinct with his report. It was then his primary duty to secure the premises until the arrival of an ambulance and detectives who would process the crime scene.

Jace photographed the body of a young woman lying on the elevator floor. In addition to noting that her head lay at an angle suggesting a broken neck, body fluids seemed minimal, indicating that the victim had been killed someplace else. Jace couldn't see any open wounds from either a gunshot or knife, and there was no evidence of any struggle because the victim looked as if she had simply fallen asleep. All of which he wrote down in his notebook.

Punching in the precinct's number on his cellphone, Jace read his findings to the officer on the desk. "Initial photos of the crime scene show the woman appears to have been attacked by someone strong enough to break her neck. I will need a team to collect any fingerprints and other matter from this scene. My partner should be here shortly. Then we'll begin interviewing possible witnesses, and hopefully find someone who knew the victim."

As he clicked off his phone, Jace greeted his partner, Bill Russell.

"I'm glad the doorman had the sense to close the doors to preserve whatever evidence we can find. After I speak with him, the resident who alerted him to the body, and gather the building video tapes for the past twenty-four hours, I'll return to the precinct."

"Yup. Standard," Bill replied.

"Bill, try to capture this woman's best image and canvas the building residents to see if anyone can ID her. I'm guessing there won't be any fingerprints on file. I checked her pockets, and they were empty. With no handbag or wallet to guide us, we have to hope she's been here before," Jace surmised.

With one more look, Jace thought not for the first time during his five years on the force, how cruel man can be. This well-dressed young woman couldn't be more than mid-twenties, pretty in a healthy way. Not a false note in her appearance. Light makeup, natural light brown hair, nails of someone who used her hands. Were the clear polish and short length due to a fashion choice or her work? *Maybe the autopsy will discover something I'm not seeing*, he thought.

Stretching his arms to loosen up his mind more than his body, Jace headed upstairs in another elevator to talk with the doorman on duty. During his earlier walk around the sub-basement and building lobby, he noticed cameras located in the back hallways, as well as in the public spaces. He also noted the camera in each elevator was located in the upper corner junction of the ceiling and wall opposite the elevator door. *Mm, full view of anyone entering or leaving the elevator*, he mused.

"I understand, Mr. Franco, that a resident alerted you to something in the elevator? Can you tell me what time that was?" Jace asked.

"Just after six this morning. I checked the monitor in elevator 3, saw the body and immediately shut it down, sent it to the sub-basement, then called the police."

"That was extremely helpful. Your swift action will help us gather information, identify this woman, and begin to search for the killer." Jace studied the young man and saw a genuine sadness in reliving the morning's events. "Was she someone you knew?" he asked quietly.

Shaking his head no, the young man paused as if he had made some decision. "Detective, this is a nice building and if someone... some stranger got into the building without my knowledge, well, I'd feel even worse than I do now."

Jace nodded. "You know, we all do what we can. But if you could keep your eyes and ears open and call me if something comes to mind, I'd appreciate it," Jace said, handing Joe Franco his card. "Now, I'll need to take those videotapes for the past twenty-four hours with me."

"All of them, not just the elevators?"

"Yes. Do you want me to speak with your building manager?"

"No. I'll let her know."

"One more item. Is the person who alerted you to the problem still in the building?"

"Yes. Mrs. Scott."

"Would you give her a call and let her know that I would like to speak with her about this morning? Please don't tell her what you found. I'll do that." Jace listened to the doorman's call and knew that he could calm a raging lunatic if needed, and was grateful for his tact.

Glancing once again at his notes, Jace wondered how someone thought they would be able to get rid of the vic without being detected. The building was only three years old, with cameras strategically placed. In addition, the doorman seemed competent, knew his responsibilities. In Jace's experience, not all buildings were as well equipped, nor employed staff that were as well trained and efficient.

Chapter 3

"So, Megan, I have most of your records. As soon as your monthly orders are gathered, give me a call and I will stop by so we can go over your accounts. Then, I'll update your numbers for quarterly taxes. They're due in a couple of weeks." Hearing her favorite client's agreement, Sally hung up and entered the conversation in her daily journal.

As she reached over for another client's file, her cell rang. It was primarily for family and friends, freeing up her home phone for business calls. "When do you have time for family, girlfriend? In fact, I'm your best friend, yet I never see you," said Jeanne, complaining in that teasing way she had.

"Right. Guilty on both accounts since you married my brother-in-law," Sally quipped. "I just get so caught up with work I forget the time, or day."

"No excuse. I'm here to rescue you. I have tomorrow off and thought since the weather is supposed to be brilliant, we could meet for lunch at the Frying Pan on the Hudson River."

"Tomorrow?" Checking her schedule, Sally thought she could push one client's pretax work to later in the day. "Absolutely, see you at noon." Clicking off the phone, Sally sat back thinking that maybe lunch with Jeanne would clear her concerns about that early morning foggy-brained vision. It remained a shadow on the edge of her mind.

As she opened the next file folder in the stack, Sally smiled with satisfaction. Everything in order. Just the way she like things. Sally loved her work as an accountant to several small businesses. But she hadn't as yet seemed to incorporate a private life into her daily schedule. After all, she was a widow, so she didn't really have a private life. And while in its third year, she was still building her roster of clients. She wasn't sure just how large a practice she wanted, just satisfied that for the present, she had everything under control.

The ringing of her home phone jolted her back to the present. "Yes?"

"Mrs. Scott, there is a Detective Logan downstairs. He asked to speak with you."

"What about, Joe?"

"This morning's elevator incident."

"But, Joe, I don't know anything. You said you were going to check things out."

"Right, and I did, and called the police. I'd rather you spoke to Detective Logan about all this."

"Okay, please tell the detective I'll be right down."

Wow, Sally thought as she saw a well-built man standing by the doorman's desk. Unlike Tyler's fashionable, crisply tailored suits, this man's navy blazer flowed over a well-toned muscular body.

"Mrs. Scott." The greeting came from a soft friendly voice, unexpected from this solidly built man.

"Yes, Detective Logan. How may I help you?"

As he led her to the sofa off to the side of the lobby, she got the feeling that what he had to say wasn't going to be pleasant.

"Joe Franco tells me you saw something in the elevator earlier today. Can you tell me what time that was and what you saw?"

"I'm rather confused. I didn't really see anything."

"The something you reported to Mr. Franco was the body of a young woman. There was no wallet or personal information found with her. Apparently, she is not a resident, so any small bit of information may help us identify her."

"How did she die?" Sally asked, now giving the man her full attention.

"We are still looking into that. The body is being taken to the morgue for a full autopsy. I'm afraid for the moment you are the only one who might give us some insight into where to begin our investigation."

"I guess you are circulating her photo," Sally surmised. The detective nodded. His seriousness confirmed her suspicions that a full-scale investigation was underway. "Well, I left my apartment at six for my morning run. The elevator opened, but I was stretching a ways down the hall and didn't get to it in time before it closed. However, as I mentioned to Joe, I saw something on the floor. It looked like bronze fabric."

"Yes, it was her coat. Do you happen to remember if the elevator was coming from one of the upper or lower floors?"

"I'm on 18, but truthfully, I didn't see the elevator indicator. If I were to guess, it was an upper floor because it came so quickly."

"The coat. Why did it catch your attention?"

"I didn't know it was a coat, but the color was an unusual bronze-brown. One of my clients owns a dress shop over on Fifth Avenue and I saw a similar fabric on one of her more expensive fashions. I think it was $800."

"That could be a good place to start. Can you give me the name of your client and the address of her shop? I'll go over personally and see what she might have to tell me about the coat. Maybe she knows the woman in our photo."

Hesitantly, Sally reached out, lightly touching the detective's arm. "May I see the photo? I mean, now that we know I saw someone, I'd like to see what she looked like."

"Of course." Running through the photos he'd taken earlier, he stopped on the one that was least traumatic. Sally studied the woman lying in a heap on the elevator floor. Pale, with light brown hair that had escaped the elastic tie at the base of her neck, she looked so peaceful.

"Does she look familiar? Maybe someone you've seen in the building?"

"I'm afraid not. Sorry, but thank you, Detective."

"Did you see anyone else leaving the building at the time you went for your run?" Jace asked.

"Not that I noticed. I'm usually focused on my route. I try to change it up to keep from getting bored. Occasionally, I'll see someone arriving or leaving. But not today." After providing the detective with Megan's information, Sally rose. "I'm afraid I have a lot of work, so if there is nothing further, I'll say goodbye."

"I may have additional questions. And I appreciate speaking to a smart woman, so if you'll give me your phone and email, next time I won't be such a surprise," he said. The upward tilt at the corner of his mouth let Sally know he would call. Maybe not entirely about the case? *Silly woman. He's just doing his job.*

Chapter 4

The entrance of the dress shop alerted Detective Logan to an upper middle-class clientele. Not the window display so much as the inviting setting where any woman who entered would expect to receive personal attention to her shopping needs.

"I'm looking for a Megan Riley," Jace said, smiling as he approached a slender woman in a fashionably tailored suit. Women he usually saw were all in pants, and this lovely lady wasn't afraid to show off her trim legs.

"Yes?" she said, giving him the once over.

"I'm Detective Jace Logan," he began, producing his shield and ID. "Mrs. Scott thought you might be able to help me identify a young woman." As he handed over his cell with the victim's photo, he saw Megan's shocked reaction with a burst of tears and a wringing of her hands.

"She's Lisa Clark, a reporter for the local newspapers. What happened? She is… was a really nice person."

"I'm sorry to have to tell you that she was found in a building elevator. You are the first person who has been able to identify her." Jace didn't want to make his questioning any more traumatic than it was seeing that Megan was clearly upset. "Can you tell me anything about her? Anything that might help us find out why she died?"

Walking over to a small office off to the side of the main showroom, Megan sat behind her desk and invited Jace to take a seat across from her. "Lisa writes profiles on small businesses here in Manhattan. She has a large following. I believe it's because of the care she takes to represent each business as unique... something her readers might want to visit." Opening a file cabinet behind her desk, she pulled out a folder and handed Jace a reprint of the profile Lisa Clark had published on her shop, Fashionably Yours.

"May I keep this?" Jace asked.

"Of course."

"When did you last see Ms. Clark?"

"I think it was two weeks or so ago. She wanted a new pair of slacks."

"Does she shop here often? Maybe one of your other customers knows her? Knows where she lived?" Jace began. Seeing the distraught store owner simply shake her head in answer to each of his questions, while holding a tissue to her eyes, he sat quietly, waiting for her to regain her composure. "Maybe there is some small bit of conversation you shared that would indicate something troubling her?" he asked quietly after seeing that the woman had once again looked his way.

Megan pushed back from her desk and closed her eyes for a moment. "I remember her telling me she was working on a story that would get her a job with *The New York Times*. That was her ambition, to work for a major newspaper."

"Did she share any of this story with you? Maybe the people involved?" Jace asked, hiding the hope that it would lead to the reason someone wanted the young woman dead.

Shaking her head, Megan's sad expression echoed in the tone of her voice. "No, she said it was about money laundering and dangerous people. That if she told me anything more, it would place me in jeopardy."

At that moment, Jace's phone rang. "Excuse me," he said as he got up and walked out of the office. It was his partner, Bill Russell. "Yes, Bill?"

"Jace, the victim is Lisa Clark, and her aunt, Mrs. Clark, is a resident in the building. I'm with her now. She was devastated seeing the photo of her niece. I simply asked for any personal information, you know, like where she lived. The basics. But it was very difficult for her to talk. Is there anything you would like me to ask her?"

"I got the same ID. You might ask how we can reach her parents, and if she had a boyfriend? Let's compare notes back at the office. We can decide our next steps then. Give Mrs. Clark your card and let her know we will be in touch, or if she thinks of anything to call you."

"Okay."

Closing his phone, Jace returned to Megan Riley's office. "Ms. Riley, I can't thank you enough for enabling us to identify

Ms. Clark. May I call if I have any further questions?" Jace asked, handing her one of his cards.

"Please do," Megan replied, and showed the detective to the shop door.

As it closed, she stood, eyes closed. I'll help this nice detective find out who did this to you, she promised.

Returning to her office, Megan quickly called Sally.

"So, the young woman is Lisa Clark, that reporter you told me wrote that glowing profile on your shop. And you told Detective Logan the coat was one she bought from you? What a small world," Sally said.

"Got to go, Sally. Stop by soon; it's been a while," Megan said.

* * *

Always busy, the precinct office that Jace shared with his team was located on an upper floor of the well-worn building. With Bill Russell and John McCauley, the third member of Jace's team, gathered round his metal desk, each began to report the results of their conversations with building residents. "It's a building of two hundred apartments, so I called John for help," Bill said and reported on those residents he had spoken with. "The only person to know the vic was her aunt."

"I reviewed the building tapes," John began. As he checked his notes, he looked up, puzzled. "In checking the elevator where the vic had been dumped or dragged, I saw a brief blackout that lasted less than a minute. But I can't seem to figure out why. However, when I checked the elevator's progress that morning, the blackout would have occurred on the twentieth floor."

"No hint of how or who placed her in the elevator?" Jace asked.

"Nope. Not a hand, face, or shadow to investigate. However, if I were to take a guess, I'd say it was a man. It would take some strength to move a body that quickly. The photos and evidence, what little there was in the elevator, are being processed. So we won't know if there were any telltale bits like fingerprints to follow up on."

"Bill, you said you spoke to the aunt? Did she have any information about the vic's family or friends?"

"A nice lady in her sixties, and married to the vic's uncle, hence the name Clark. Horrified is too mild for her reaction to the photo of her niece. I remember her saying that she was the only family the girl had. That her parents had died a few years before in a car crash. And, as far as she knew didn't have a boyfriend."

"Anything else that might give us a leg up in our investigation?" Jace asked.

"Mrs. Clark told me that Lisa said she was working on some high-profile crime for a possible book. When I asked for additional details, she just shook her head. Then said she wanted to help us solve her niece's murder and went to her handbag on a nearby table, where she took two keys off her key chain and gave them to me. She said they were to Lisa's apartment and then wrote out her address. I remember the hopeful look she gave me. It made me want to work even harder to find the murderer. I did tell her that we would need to restrict access to the apartment for a while. She was more than willing to accommodate us. That's all of it," Bill reported.

"Okay, next steps. John and Bill, we have to visit the vic's apartment," Jace instructed. "Let's start now."

Chapter 5

Wearing a colorful sundress, Sally walked a little over a mile to the Hudson River and one of her favorite outdoor spots since she moved into the city. It was a pier and restored lightship turned into a restaurant frequented at night by the city's young professionals. During the week, it was a haven away from honking horns and concrete, with green grass and trees reminiscent of her former life in the suburbs.

Hugs and kisses brought smiles from both Sally and Jeanne. "I missed you so much," Jeanne began. "I want to hear all about you – any new clients? What you do with your free time. Everything," she said enthusiastically.

"Ladies," the waiter greeted them as he approached their outdoor table on the side of the pier. "Let me explain the menu scan on the sign. You can open it on your phone, read the full menu of selections, and enter your order."

"Is this another COVID mandate or a technology upgrade?" Sally asked. "We're outdoors in case anyone is checking." Sally hated doing things on computers, as she spent all day on hers. With the sweetest of smiles, she looked up at the young waiter. "Couldn't we just give you our orders instead of this automated thing?"

The young man, looking amused, replied, "It will be my pleasure. What can I get you?"

"We'll take two Long Island Ice Teas, and when you get back, you might give us an idea of items on your menu," Jeanne said. With a nod in agreement, the waiter left them and Jeanne began to fill Sally in on her life as Mrs. Ryan Scott. "… and Ryan got me to reduce my hours at the hospital. When I told him I'd be earning less, he asked me if I worked for the money or love of what I did. Isn't he wonderful? When I responded that I loved helping the patients resolve their after-care and financial problems, I realized I could do that on a reduced schedule. So now I work a three-day week."

"Oh, Jeanne, he's so right for you. Ryan knows you want to help people, but I think he wants more of your time. He's been widowed for so long. Maybe that's why he always worked so hard," Sally mused.

"He does," Jeanne said with a dreamy look.

Sally could see her best friend's happiness. "I'm glad you and Ryan eloped last December. I've never seen either of you so content."

"Enough about me. Why has it taken you three years to settle into your new life in the city? When you had the house in suburbia, you at least called to say hello," Jeanne scolded.

"You don't understand. When I moved into the apartment, I had two clients… the Golf Club and Megan's dress shop. And, while it met my basic financial needs, I didn't have the professional setup a business requires. You know, to look expert without having a large office and staff. I didn't want to look like an amateur. Remember, I still had to finish up my degree and take my CPA exam. I was busy."

"You set up other people's businesses. So what was different in organizing yours? And now with this pandemic, more people are working from home, so it should be especially easy for you."

"A fully designed website, stationary, folios for proposals and reports. And my own set of books. But it was getting accustomed to the ritual of recording every conversation and decision made that took time to get accustomed to. Now it reminds me of the work I did before Tyler and I married, when I was his executive assistant," Sally said and quickly took a sip of her drink. "Then there was the apartment. Setting it up, and as my budget allowed, purchasing needed bits of this or that."

"And that has taken three years? It's a two-bedroom apartment, not a whole house," Jeanne cried in disbelief.

"The first year to make sure I handled those two clients expertly. The second to sign more clients, and now the third when I am finally secure, I'm in the midst of a murder investigation."

"Murder?" Jeanne all but yelled.

"I was going for a morning jog and saw something in the elevator before it shut in my face. Turns out it was a murdered woman, and a Detective Logan questioned me about what I saw. Just filling in details to help his investigation. But I don't really know what help I've been."

"You said he asked you a lot of questions."

"Apparently, I know more than I thought I did. For instance, I identified the coat she was wearing as one in Megan's shop. He also asked if I knew anything about her. Stuff like that."

"And this detective? What's he like?" Jeanne asked, suspecting that Sally was holding something back.

"Jeanne, unlike my sophisticated husband, this man is a hunk… not in a bodybuilding kind of way, just solid, without an ounce to spare." As if an afterthought, she added, "He thinks I'm smart."

Jeanne sat quietly, watching her best friend come to life before her eyes. "Sally, what are you doing next weekend? Why not let me arrange for Ryan to get Billy and Judy from that shrew Tyler divorced, and with Jane and Mark, we can all take a trip out to the beach? Hot dogs, hamburgers, bathing suits and we can get you away from your self-imposed isolation."

"That's just what I need. A dose of laughter, boisterous kids, and fun. But why not go to my mom's in New Jersey? She lives near the shore and would love the chance to pamper her grandchildren. She now has four, thanks to my marrying into the Scott family. The kids adore her, and she can arrange for a backyard barbeque… and even put us all up. The kids can bunk in the TV Room, and you and Ryan in my old bedroom, and I can sleep on the sofa in the living room."

"Oh, Sally, that would be wonderful. You know, what I also love about my husband is the attention he pays to Tyler's kids. Somehow, he's been able to get them released from that bitch's custody and visit us in the city. As long as he doesn't mention you… the woman who stole her husband. Victoria has backed off and even lets us keep them for full weekends at a time. We may be a jigsaw kind of family, but we are a loving one," Jeanne said.

"Terrific. I'll call Mom when I get back. Just give me a time and I'll meet you downstairs." Sally hadn't felt as light and happy in more than three years. Lunch was delicious, and picking up where she and Jeanne had left off all those months ago while sipping her second Long Island Ice Tea, fully mellowed her out.

On her way home, the photo of the murdered young girl flashed in her mind. The good mood from her time with Jeanne vanished. *One day at a time. I'll get through this the same way I survived Tyler's death.*

Chapter 6

"Two more tax returns to go," Sally said, satisfied with her progress. In three years, her first two clients had become friends, and she was able to help them with tips on organization along with managing the all-important profit and loss issues that would arise. It was the kind of business relationship she valued. The additional four clients had been the result of referrals. She had studied them as carefully as they did her capabilities. Sitting back in her chair, she smiled with satisfaction at what she had built. Financially independent and living on her own. And at thirty-two, finally feeling she was in control of her life.

The jarring of the phone brought her back to the present. "Hello," a distracted Sally said, her thoughts focused on her successful business.

"Mrs. Scott, this is Detective Logan. I hope I'm not interrupting anything, but I was wondering if we could meet. Not entirely about the case. More out of curiosity. Mine. You seem to have a good sense of the activities in your building. I'd love to hear more about your day-to-day life."

"I will be finishing up by five-thirty."

"Why don't you let me buy you a drink? It's the least I can do for the help you have given me with this investigation."

Was this dream of a man asking her out? Of course not. She was a widow, not a young woman. "Is this an official visit?" she asked with a chuckle, perking up on hearing his laughter.

"No, this is on me. If you don't mind, that is," Jace replied.

"That would be very nice. How about meeting me downstairs at six?"

* * *

The pastel pink cotton sundress floated around Sally as she walked up to Detective Logan, and seeing his appreciative smile, eased some of her jitters. *Silly. It's just business. But I can still enjoy his company.*

"I thought we'd stop at Pete's Tavern. It's nearby and livelier than the building lobby," he began, and guided her down the street.

"Would you believe I've lived here for three years and never been there," Sally said.

As they entered the noisy bar inside the entrance of the famous neighborhood restaurant, Detective Logan asked for a booth in the back. Fortunately, there was one available.

"The back is somewhat quieter. And, it's also frowned on for me to be seen fraternizing with a witness," he whispered near Sally's ear, then stepped aside and waited for Sally to follow the restaurant manager threading his way through the bar crowd to a backroom booth.

Settled, Sally sat looking around the pub-like room with a chalkboard listing the evening's specials.

"This tavern has been around since the late 1800s but was purchased in 1922 and renamed Pete's Tavern. It's famous for being the place where O'Henry wrote his stories, as well as being located near Tammany Hall, a major political entity in New York City politics at that time," Jace said.

"To be honest, when I moved into my building, I selected it for its neighborhood feel, away from the hustle and bustle of midtown. But I haven't really explored the area, other than jogging around Gramercy Park."

"May I take your orders?" the young woman asked, looking over at Sally. "Can you make a sidecar?" Seeing the surprise on Logan's face, she quickly added, "I haven't had one in a very long time."

"Make that two," Logan said.

When the drinks arrived, he raised his glass. "To my favorite witness. Generous with her time and thoughts."

As she sipped her drink, Sally couldn't decide if she liked being called a witness. "Actually, I'm more of an onlooker," she corrected.

"Okay, onlooker. I'm curious about the building," Jace said, and took a sip of his drink. "And, by the way, your client was able to identify our unfortunate young woman. Her name is Lisa Clark."

Sally nodded. "Yes, Megan told me about your visit."

"Well, since Ms. Clark's aunt lives in your building and she had visited her on occasion, she would be familiar to the doormen on duty. So would he have to announce her arrival?"

"He would still call up, and when given approval by Mrs. Clark, admit her."

"Even if she had been to the building many times before?"

"Yes. I've found that when people live in close proximity, they never just ring someone's bell. The doorman announces them. That is one of this city's bit of manners I particularly appreciate. It makes me feel safe, not like living alone in a big house where just anyone could walk up to your door and ring your bell."

"But could someone sneak into the building unobserved? I noticed cameras throughout the building, and in each elevator."

"Actually, with the recent increase in people ordering things online, the doormen are frequently busy checking in packages and are not focused on the building cameras. So, yes, I guess someone knowing how to divert their attention could enter unobserved." The wrinkled brow showed Sally wasn't happy with that thought.

"Do you know Mrs. Clark? I believe she lives on the fifth floor?"

"Not really know her. I sometimes pass her in the lobby, or meet her in the laundry room. We exchange brief comments, you know about the weather, the latest building breakdown. Or compliments about the way she looks. Stuff like that."

Having barely touched her drink, Sally took a sip and looked up. "Detective—"

"Please call me Jace. Remember, I'm off duty," he said with a conspirator's grin.

"—Jace. Can you tell me anything about Ms. Clark? Why she was killed? I'd rather think of her as a living flesh and blood person than a corpse. So, any little thing about her would help."

"You deserve at least that. Apparently, Lisa Clark was an up-and-coming reporter. She writes a weekly column for the neighborhood newspapers about places and happenings around the city. And, I understand, is sometimes called in by the local news networks to fill in on a story."

"Reporter. Right. Megan told me a little while ago that someone had written a really nice article on her shop and it brought in new customers. It must have been Ms. Clark, and that's why she knew her a bit better than just someone who bought a coat from her."

After a thoughtful sip, Sally's curiosity got the better of her. "Another question. Why are you so interested in my building? It must be like all other high-rises in the city."

"Each building has its own personality. So while they may be run in similar fashion, I've found the residents know more about what is going on than the management. In your case, when you sent me to your client's dress shop, you gave me the first break in the case… Lisa Clark's identity."

"Did you talk to each of my neighbors? Was her aunt the only other person to identify her?"

"My team spoke to whoever was available that morning. So far, your client and Mrs. Clark are the only two to have known her. We will be following up with others if it becomes necessary."

"If it becomes necessary? I don't understand."

"Usually, and no two cases are exactly the same, once we identify the victim, we look into their life. We try to find out who may have wanted to do them harm. But the first most important bit of information, other than results of the autopsy, is to identify the victim."

Pleased to know she had helped, Sally raised her glass. "To finding the killer. I'll help if I can."

Chapter 7

"Okay, guys, where do we stand?" Jace asked as Bill and John joined him around his desk. Coffee cups, notepads, and pens at the ready.

"John, I've done as you suggested and reviewed the tapes from the elevator camera. You're right, something got in the way so we can't identify the person or persons who placed the body in the elevator."

"What could black out a camera?" John asked. "Surveillance is my area, and I found the cameras all in working order. When I went back to look at the one in that elevator, there was nothing sprayed on the lens to limit coverage. But on the videotape, for a brief forty seconds, it was totally black. It's like a magician had covered the lens with a black cloth."

"I saw that… but also tracked all four of the elevators, trying to find the time the vic entered one to visit her aunt. That was at four-fifteen the day before finding her body. But, when I saw her get back into an elevator three hours later, she didn't go down to the lobby. No, she got off at the fifteenth floor. I couldn't see where she went. So, John, pull up the names of residents on that floor and see if they rent or own their apartments, where they work, anything that might indicate someone our vic would want to visit," Jace instructed.

"Bill, anything new from the other tenants?" Jace asked.

"Still nothing there. Only my initial conversation with the aunt."

"Continue checking into the young woman's life. Driver's license, credit cards, bank accounts. You might want to call the aunt and see if there was anyone she had problems with. A former boyfriend, someone at work? Or places she frequented, like a bar or restaurant. Yesterday's search of her apartment did turn up a computer, flash drives, and even her file cabinet. But the folders seem to cover her past articles. Why not see if they contain any leads. Something related to that book she was researching. According to Megan Riley, it was about money laundering," Jace reported. "That would suggest large sums being earned illegally."

"I checked with the tech guys," John said. "They're working as fast as possible, but are swamped with another ongoing case. It's going to take some time. But, funny thing, if I were working on something sensitive, I'd back it up, or at least keep it in a separate location. And we didn't find any other hiding places."

"I watched you tear apart every drawer and cabinet in the place. I can't imagine we missed anything. Go back to the lab and ask the computer experts where they might hide information they didn't want found on a computer. Maybe we should take another look," Jace added.

"Bill, also follow up with her employer. She might have been assigned that story to start with. Tomorrow we'll regroup and see where we stand. I'm afraid if we don't get any leads, we'll have to check out the apartment again," Jace said.

When Bill and John left, Jace turned on his computer. "Sally Scott, are you too good to be true? Is there anything I should be aware of? Boyfriends? Children? Could you simply be a nice, pretty… no, very pretty young woman?"

As Jace entered Sally's name into the search bar, he saw that Scott was a relatively common name. Hitting escape, he decided it would be more interesting to find out who Sally was in person.

* * *

It had been a surprising evening, Sally thought. Jace Logan had said he was breaking official rules to take her out for a drink. *Yeah, and pump me for information about the building. Why does that bother me so much?*

She wasn't going to be able to sleep until she had sorted out the questions she had about Lisa Clark's murder. As she often did when trying to puzzle out a problem, Sally pulled out a lined pad and began to doodle circles and lines that began to transform into words. *Should I be nervous because I discovered the body? Who in the building, other than her aunt, might have known her? Should I question Allison or Mildred about the neighbors on their floors just above and below mine? If I know most of the people on eighteen, they will probably know most everyone on theirs. While we are friends, I have to be careful and come up with some subterfuge and not reveal my connection to the police investigation. They might not even know there has been a murder in the building.*

* * *

Awake early, Sally was sitting at the kitchen counter with her first cup of coffee for the day. The pad with last evening's notes sat within reach. Heavily underlined were the words *be careful,* and she pushed the pad away. Where to begin? Home base? Who might be a bit different? Stand out from the predominantly middle-class people living in her building?

Picking up her toast from the toaster, she automatically buttered it and spooned on some jam. Her mind tried to visualize the building's residents she had either seen or had some relationship with. No one stood out.

I can't ask Joe. He's already warned me that management doesn't want him sharing tidbits of information about residents.

Once again reaching for her notepad, Sally added Allison and Mildred's names under a new heading: PEOPLE TO TALK TO ABOUT NOTICING ANYONE STRANGE ON THEIR FLOORS.

Chapter 8

Every time Sally walked into Fashionably Yours, she slowed her pace, and listened to the soft sound of music that hung in the air, enjoying the escape from Fifth Avenue's noise of horns, sirens, and ambulances that regularly assaulted her when out on the city streets.

"Hi, Sally," greeted the willowy brunette dressed in a smart lavender linen pantsuit. "I'm all ready for you. Let's go back into my office and I'll pour you a glass of ice tea. It's blueberry today."

"I love coming here and probably should pay you for the sense of luxury and peace you've incorporated into the store."

As she handed Sally a file folder, Megan took out another file from her desk. "Here are my projected earnings for the rest of the year. I've kept them separate because I need your opinion as to whether my latest idea is worth the added investment."

"I will certainly give your plan serious thought and call you tomorrow. We can explore your ideas then," Sally said before placing the folder in her briefcase. As she looked back at Megan, she smiled. "I also think you're ready to develop new prospects. This isn't upper Fifth Avenue; you might consider expanding to Chelsea or NoHo." Sally could see how pleased her friend was to hear her mention expanding her business. Megan was a delight as a client because she watched every penny going in and out, so when she decided to spend, it wasn't a rash decision.

"Okay, now if you will just sign this release that gives me permission to file your quarterly tax returns electronically, I think we're done," Sally said.

"And here is your ice tea. It comes from that little tea shop around the corner, just in case it's something you like," Megan said, topping off Sally's glass with a sprig of mint.

"Megan, Detective Logan tells me you gave him a copy of that article Lisa Clark wrote about the shop. That it gave a fabulous boost to business. I know you've told me about her in the past. But, now, can you tell me what she was like? Having never met her, I somehow feel responsible." Hearing Megan take a breath, she quickly added, "No, not about her death. But maybe to find answers so the detectives can find her killer."

"She was like a spring day. Upbeat, fresh-faced, and engaging, but quiet. And she came into the shop the first week I opened. I was drawn to her because her questions were about more than my fashions, but my philosophy. You know, *you should be your own best friend and buy something that makes you smile. A scarf, belt, or that special dress to make your husband sit up and take notice.* Better yet, we became friends."

"Do you have any idea who would want to kill her? It was quite a shock to know that the piece of fabric on the elevator floor was actually a murdered woman. I've always felt safe in my building. Now I'm not so sure."

"Sally, Lisa was researching a major money laundering scam for a book she was writing. I did tell that to Detective Logan. But why are you interested in Lisa?" Megan asked.

"Money laundering? That is something I could look into… what is the saying? 'Follow the money?'"

"Why would you want to look into what must be a dangerous story? On the other hand, I know Lisa was a smart young woman with a future in investigative journalism. I'd love to help them catch the criminal."

"How much trouble can I get into by looking things up on my computer?" Sally said, hoping to take Megan's mind off her murdered friend.

"Another topic," Sally began. "I'm going to visit my mom with the Scott clan and would love something that didn't spell hermit. Do you have anything that might make me look like I was enjoying myself?"

"Why do you always sell yourself short? And, yes, I have the perfect white denim pants and tunic top in your pastel colors. You seem to always dress in a gray top and pants. No wonder you forgot you're a young, attractive woman."

Laughing felt good. "Haven't you heard? Gray is the new black," Sally quipped.

"Black isn't any better," Megan replied.

Chapter 9

The front door of the colonial house was flung open and Barbara Compton stood with arms open wide to welcome a laughing group of children and adults. One by one, the boisterous kids rushed in for their hugs. For Billy and Judy, the only hugs they ever got were from their uncle, Ryan, his new wife, Jeanne, and their stepmother, Sally. While they knew that their mother, Victoria, hated Sally, they remembered visiting their father and his new wife, clinging to memories of those brief visits for the warmth and love they didn't have at home. Now, along with their cousins, Jane and Mark, they too looked forward to being pampered by the grandmotherly Barbara. She was always ready to listen, bake their favorite cookies, not to mention give hugs. Lots of hugs.

"Okay, Scott Family," Barbara greeted. "Drop your stuff in the den; we can sort you all out later. For now, kids, the badminton net is up and equipment on the backyard table. Grownups, join me in the kitchen."

"Mom, when did you become such a dictator?" asked Sally with a laugh.

"When I became a grandmother... at last." The good-natured kidding was welcomed by Ryan, who had raised his younger brother Tyler when their parents had been killed, and never had a sense of family until his marriage and the birth of his daughter and son. Just as his growing family was enjoying their lives, his wife died from cancer, leaving him to deal with another major loss. And now, with his marriage to Jeanne, Ryan had that happy family. Barbara completed the multigenerational group for which he was eternally grateful.

"Barbara, I've adopted you along with Jane and Mark," Ryan said, enveloping this kindly woman in a bear hug. He felt her pats on his back that almost brought tears.

Jeanne moved in for her hug. "Barbara, I've finally gotten to know you and love you like everyone else," she said, meaning every word. As Sally's former roommate, and now sister-in-law, she loved the way Barbara had been embraced by the whole family.

Later, after the kids had gone inside for video games, Barbara brought out a bottle of wine and nibbles of cheese and crackers, setting the tray on the garden table. "Mom, I don't remember ever having such a nice summer evening when growing up," Sally said.

"Well, you were busy, then your father passed away and I guess I just withdrew." Looking at her daughter with a warm smile, she added, "You know, kiddo, your own grief brought me out of my shell. And look around you. See the gifts your marriage to Tyler gave us all."

"To the Scott's newest member, Barbara," Ryan said, raising his glass in the toast.

"Thank you. Being surrounded by your loving smiles couldn't make me happier."

Conversation flowed as each shared their latest news, until Jeanne blurted out, "Have you heard about Sally's murder?" Seeing the horror on Barbara's face, Jeanne quickly looked over at Sally and saw that she hadn't shared this bit of news with her mother.

"Sally?" Barbara inquired as quietly as she could, her silent fury clearly evident on her scowling face.

"Mom, there isn't anything to tell. I was going for a morning run, thought I'd seen something in the elevator that had closed in my face, and it turned out to be a murdered woman." *Well, that's about as succinctly as I could have told it.*

"Apparently there's more to it than that," Barbara said, now in full motherly mode.

"Actually, I was going to ask Ryan how to research something. Now that everyone is in the loop, Ryan, how would I find out about running a money laundering scheme on a relatively large scale?" Silence descended on the group.

"Sally, why would you want information on a criminal enterprise?" Ryan asked in his usual quiet way.

"I'm rather good at numbers. And it seems that the victim was working on a story about a criminal enterprise. Since I know how to do things legally to protect my clients, I wondered how a criminal would launder large amounts of money? Are we talking offshore bank accounts? Trucking bills into the country?

What?" Seeing the shock on her mother's face, she quickly added, "I'm curious, that's all. They didn't teach me that at university."

"Well, it is getting harder to keep the government out of money transfers larger than, say, ten thousand dollars. I guess you should check the business library and see if there is a recent book on the topic," Ryan replied.

"On TV cop shows, they hide value in gemstones," Jeanne said.

"Ah ha," was all Sally said. She'd have to find the answers on her own. Her family didn't seem to support her curiosity about the murdered young woman's research.

Sally had a sudden feeling of emptiness. Jeanne had Ryan, Jane, and Mark. Even her love for her step kids, Judy and Billy, couldn't fill the void. Ever since the courts denied her custody, the poor kids remained with their mother, one of the coldest women Sally had ever met. The laughter and warmth of the day brought back memories she had tried to erase. Tyler and his kids, Ryan and his kids… family. It had been all she had ever wanted.

* * *

After deciding she no longer wanted to stay over at her mother's house, she took a train home and was now standing in front of her open apartment door. It usually gave her a sense of wellbeing. As Sally stood looking into her long living room so neat and tidy, she wished there were kids' toys to pick up from the floor, or a sweater tossed on a chair. The little things she dreamed about in the silence of the night. Instead, here she was, the lonely aunt. She felt like an outsider.

"Oh well," she murmured. Instead of heading to the bedroom to get ready for bed, she looked at her watch and saw that it was only ten. Dropping her keys on the table by the front door, Sally headed into the kitchen where she pulled an open bottle of Chardonnay from the fridge and poured it into one of her larger wine glasses. The glass was part of a set Jeanne had given her as a wedding gift when she and Tyler married. As she was about to take that first sip, tears formed.

Shit. Quickly wiping away the tears, she looked at the glass. This is becoming a habit, she thought and, ignoring her cautionary thoughts, took her first sip, fortifying herself for the empty hours ahead.

Chapter 10

The day loomed brightly in Sally's home office, a promising start. As she sorted through her stack of folders set aside for the day's work, a sudden thought crossed her mind. If these were records of someone laundering money from illegal activities, how would they be recorded?

Remembering what she had told her mother the night before, "I'm just curious," was in part true. *Hell, a hard-working young woman was murdered in my building; I have to find out why.*

Her first thought was to search the internet for information on money laundering. Most of what this cursory search came up with was a simple definition: 'Hiding the origins of money illegally obtained.'

Sitting back, she tried to think of all the news reports, TV crime shows, and novels she'd read and decided illegal businesses could mean drugs, sex trafficking, or extortion.

"I'm not even capable of planning a fake enterprise based on any of these businesses," she mumbled. "But if someone in this building had extensive business interests that hid nefarious activities, they might resort to laundering their ill-gotten gains."

The building was only three years old, and she was one of the original tenants, having moved in before the building had been completed. She thought she'd recognize most all residents, even if she didn't know where they lived or their names. "Okay, let's do this," she said as she picked up her phone to call one of her neighbors on nineteen, the floor above.

"Hi, Allison, Sally here. Am I calling at a bad time?"

"No, just pouring my morning coffee. Wait, I'll be right back…. I'm back, what's up? Scheduling a lunch date?"

"No. I was just wondering if you knew everyone living on your floor."

"Not really, why? And don't give me your usual 'Y is a crooked letter,'" Allison said with a chuckle.

"What I'm wondering is if in this building of mostly single, retired, and senior citizens, you knew of any well-heeled businessmen that weren't particularly friendly."

"Friendly? This building is filled with friendlies, mainly people with manners. Do you mean anyone I'd think odd?"

"Exactly."

"What has you investigating our building residents, anyway?" Allison asked.

"Well, I'm working with a client and she was interested in our building. She asked what kind of people lived here. Of course, I raved about you and so I thought to ask if there was anyone strange on your floor. Someone who didn't look quite legit."

"Let me think. No, there isn't anyone who looks suspicious."

"Thanks, Allison. Give me a couple of weeks to get past tax season, then I'll call you about lunch."

Next, the twentieth floor at the top of the building. "Hello, Mildred? Sally. Hope I'm not interrupting anything."

"Sally, where have you been? It's like you just dropped off the face of the earth."

"Tax season. Anyway, the reason I'm calling is a client of mine was interested in knowing more about the people in our building. She said she may want her niece to move into a one-bedroom. I gave her the usual overview: singles, a few young families, retired, etc. Then I wondered if anyone on your floor looked different."

"Different? You mean from our middle-class mainstream?"

"Yes. I've seen young women who look like models visiting someone in the building, so maybe someone in show business, or publishing?"

"I've seen those girls and every time I wish I'd renewed my gym membership," Mildred sighed. "But to your question, there is one man who usually leaves the building when I'm getting home at five. He's sort of rough looking but dressed in Zenga suits."

"Do you know what he does? His name?" Sally was hoping she may have found one person to research instead of theories.

"I think he owns several restaurants, and by his clothes they must have expensive menus. Zenga suits are in the finest of fabrics, with prices starting at $6,000. That's way more than my monthly maintenance bills," Mildred added, laughing at the thought.

"Great, and yes, I will call you when taxes are done," Sally said as she hung up the phone. *Now what?*

* * *

Sally waited until five p.m. the following day before heading down to the lobby for her mail. As she stepped from the elevator, she saw a well-dressed man passing the doorman. "Hey, Sam, can you tell me who that man is? I think I saw his photo in some magazine," Sally said.

"Sure, Mrs. Scott. That's Robert Maffeo."

Nodding her thanks, Sally headed back to the elevator and home to research Mr. Maffeo when something prickled the skin on the back of her neck. Slowly looking around the building lobby, she couldn't see anyone or anything out of place. Just nerves, she decided and continued on her way.

Chapter 11

A glass of wine to complete my day? Of course, Sally decided as she went to her fridge in search of an opened bottle of her favorite Chardonnay. "I guess a new bottle is in order," she mumbled as she opened the adjoining cabinet.

With her first sip, curiosity about the well-dressed Robert Maffeo returned. Booting up her computer, she decided to first look at Lisa Clark's columns, wanting to see who the young woman covered in her two years of reporting on neighborhood businesses.

A photo of Lisa Clark embellished her website, along with an index of her articles. The photo was that of a young, pleasantly smiling woman. Not a studio shot. It looked like it had been taken on a cellphone by a friend. Scrolling through her articles, Sally spotted Megan's store and, sipping her wine, read the reporter's view of Megan's business. "Well, you do have a talent for personalizing your subjects. I agree with Megan; you captured her philosophy perfectly."

Next, she again scanned the index, spotting Maffeo's name. "So, it looks like you can afford $6,000 suits," Sally said, surprised by the extent of the man's restaurant empire. He had several Italian restaurants in each of the five boroughs, and one highly rated upscale dining emporium located in the

Lincoln Center area. An area of tourists and well-heeled patrons of the famous performing arts center for ballet, opera, and symphony productions.

"Maybe Jeanne will join me for dinner and we can scope you out," she mused as she dialed her cell. "Hi, Jeanne, hope I'm not interrupting your dinner preparations," Sally began.

"Not quite yet. It's a simple casserole tonight and all it needs is time in the oven. What's up?"

"How would you like to go on a scouting mission tomorrow night at an expensive Lincoln Center restaurant? Say around 6:30?"

"Scouting? Give. What are you really up to?"

"There's a man in my building who is somewhat of a mystery. I just wanted to see if he is all that special as reported in a recent article I've read."

"And why this particular man? A possible romantic interest?" Jeanne's hopeful voice had Sally chuckling. "Stop it! No. It's about that murder. I'll fill you in tomorrow night over drinks and dinner."

* * *

"Sally, you look wonderful," Jeanne said as she hugged her best friend in front of a busy street-level restaurant. As she looked in the windows, she whispered more to herself, "I wonder what this dinner is going to cost us? Not that Ryan ever complains about my credit card charges."

"By now, he is probably accustomed to your living on a rather sensible budget, one dictated by your modest hospital salary. I doubt he'll even mention it," Sally said, trying to ease her friend's moment of concern and remembering that she, too, had been aware of every penny she spent. *Now it's every dollar.* The thought brought a smile of satisfaction.

"You're right. Tonight it's all about snooping," Jeanne replied.

"I just hope the food is up to the reviews, and prices. I checked the menu and I expect with drinks and three courses it will be the most expensive charge on my credit card this month," Sally said.

With laughter fueling their entrance to Maffeo's, a model in the latest figure-hugging dress greeted them and escorted Sally and Jeanne to a table off to the side of the main dining room.

"Okay, one question answered," Sally said as she picked up the menu. "How about a real drink? Tonight is a girls' night out."

The waiter left with their drink orders and Jeanne prompted, "What explains what question?"

"It seems that Mr. Robert Maffeo is quite a mystery in my building. My upstairs neighbor, Mildred, says he usually leaves around five in the evening and is often seen with a gorgeous model on his arm. Since there are multiple women, I'm thinking they may work for him as hostesses in one of his restaurants."

"So, he's suspect because he is more Hollywood than Manhattan?"

"Sort of." With their drinks sitting before them, Sally raised her glass. "To us."

"I'll always drink to that," Jeanne replied.

"Now for dinner?" Sally said as she began to go over the menu. "Well, pumpkin stuffed ravioli with basil butter is a far cry from meatballs and spaghetti."

"Did you see the other appetizers? Grilled octopus, well that's rarely well prepared. Skewered shrimp with leeks and olives. Oh, and my favorite, stuffed clams," Jeanne read.

"Let's order the octopus and clams and share," Sally said, and seeing Jeanne's agreement, returned to the main course selections. "I see what I want… Zuppa di Pesci. The seafood alone will tell us if this has a Michelin quality kitchen."

"I've never had sweet and sour tuna steaks. Maybe I should try something out of my comfort zone," Jeanne said, looking at Sally for approval.

"Why not, and we can share."

The young man returned to their table. "May I get you another drink, ladies?"

"Yes, please," Sally replied, "and we'd like to place our orders."

As Sally gave their orders for appetizers and the main course, it occurred to her she might see if she could copy the fish soup. It would make a wonderful family dinner. In the three years she had only had one dinner party, and that was to thank Jeanne, Ryan, and her mother for standing by her during the days before and after Tyler's funeral.

Settled with their refills, Sally looked around the main dining room and spotted her neighbor going from table to table. It looked to her that many were repeat customers, as Mr. Maffeo seemed to linger at some of the tables. But his charm eluded her. Watching him as he worked the room, she decided maybe he had secrets. If not money laundering, maybe a double set of books?

"Don't stare, but see that man over there by the window table with four well-dressed people? The one in the perfectly tailored suit?" Sally asked.

Noticing that Jeanne had located the man, Sally sat back. "Do you think this smooth host is really a rough customer underneath his perfect wardrobe? Or, actually legit?"

"And you were thinking he could be behind the murdered woman?" Jeanne asked in hushed tones.

"Maybe. But maybe not. He's just … so cliché. You know, someone born poor and made good." Smiling across the table, Sally sipped her drink. "I'll have to rethink my assumptions. Let's just enjoy our meal."

Chapter 12

Sally was dressed for her meeting with Indigo, one of New York's best-kept secrets, a southern baker who had charmed SoHo residents for the past two years. Indigo was one of Sally's newer clients and had been recommended by a neighbor who had fallen in love with her southern sweets, including butterscotch nuggets, and pecan pie with more pecans than filler.

Giving herself one more look in the mirror, Sally wanted to dress in the spirit of the bakery. While the dessert selections were as lovely to look at as delectable to taste, the décor was Southern Tea Room, complete with tablecloths and china service. Her white skirt and colorful cotton blouse fit the bill. "Not a cold Manhattanite, but a lady," Sally remarked and laughed. "Polite, maybe, but a lady? I'm not that old."

The empty elevator greeted Sally, who was lost in thought about her upcoming meeting. So, when it stopped a few floors below and she was joined by a well-groomed older woman and tall man in his fifties, she did what she always did; she greeted her neighbors. "Good morning," Sally said.

"Good morning," the older woman replied, remaining focused on the elevator doors. The man only nodded.

So much for morning conversation. He isn't much better… whoever he is.

When the elevator reached the lobby, Sally stood aside and watched the woman take the younger man's arm and head for the building's entrance. She had only seen them a few times since she moved in. What was comforting was that they were always together, and that she seemed to rely on him for support. Thinking about the two, Sally decided there was something old-fashioned in not only their dress, but their way of keeping to themselves. Certainly unlike any of the other tenants she knew in the building, always ready for a quick, chatty greeting.

And here I'm looking for people who stand out in the building, Sally thought. *Those two try very hard to disappear. I wonder why? Who are they? Something to check out.*

Passing the doorman's station, she stopped. "Hi, Joe, can you tell me the names of the two people that just left the building?"

"Sure, they moved in about the same time you did. It's Mrs. Rafkin, and Mr. Rafkin."

"Thanks," she said as she left the building wondering, *Mr. Rafkin… son, nephew? I can't worry about them now. They look harmless.*

* * *

"Indigo, every time I visit, I swear I've put on an extra five pounds," Sally said, greeting the twenty-five-year-old standing behind a glass case filled with cupcakes, pies, and more sugar than Sally had seen in years.

"Miss Sally, if I may be so rude, you could use an extra pound or two. And I am going to help by packing up some of your favorites."

"I'm not going to refuse. I love your creations. And I'm here with my latest for you. I've done a half-year review and you will be delighted to know that your sales have increased 25 percent over the same time last year."

"Oh. I knew I was doing well, but not that well. It's the new building around the corner. It's filled with young tech workers. They stop by on their way to work and pick up something with their coffee," Indigo replied, a pleased expression highlighting her high cheekbones and brown tinted skin. "To think I won't have to go home. I guess the ads are right. If you can make it here, you can make it anywhere." Laughing at the oft-used expression in praise of New York City, the two women settled at a table at the back of the store. While Indigo set a carrot muffin on Sally's plate, Sally was busy pulling out a folder and turning on her laptop.

"So, which do you want first? Sales or profits?" Sally asked, her smile telling Indigo that she'd be pleased with both.

"Everything. Oh, and should I hire another sales clerk? That way, I can add new desserts to my offerings."

"Well, let's see where you are, and I may have an idea to help increase sales," Sally said and the two women sat with heads close, all sounds of the city, even the arrival of customers, ignored.

* * *

Later, on her arrival at home, Sally's mind returned to the older woman and her companion. Making a cup of coffee, she booted up her computer and typed Rafkin in the search box.

There was a Rafkin and Sons Antiquarian Bookstore with a web address. Clicking on that, she viewed a staid, black and white graphic that looked like a copper plate announcement with the name of the store, a phone number, and a small photo of an elderly man in the lower right-hand corner. The photo looked almost like an afterthought. The following page contained photos showing the store's interior, featuring an open central part of the room. The perimeter contained glass display cases, and along the opposite wall were a few cubicles with tables and chairs for two people. Nothing in the display cases was clearly visible. Hanging on the walls behind the counter were framed documents and maps that looked like they had come from a museum. On the third and last page was a note designed like an old-fashioned calling card that read, 'By Appointment Only', and again listed a phone number. *Funny. No address or owner listed. Well, well. Very understated. Just like Mrs. Rafkin.*

Her own business world was more inventive with business owners developing creatively designed websites showcasing information about their company's services, listing of recommendations, and the all-important contact page for inquiries. So, while Rafkin and Sons projected a staid image, she didn't think there was anything that hinted of a criminal enterprise.

Chapter 13

It had been a hell of a couple of days. All but one of her client's taxes were ready to send to the IRS and NYS. She just needed Freddy's. And before she could finalize them, she had to remind him to tighten up his record keeping. The beauty salon used paper tickets for each of their clients. Each ticket detailed the services purchased, and it was those she used to record his sales. But lately the tickets hadn't been complete. *Okay, Freddy, I know you're busy, but I will have to visit in person.*

Dialing his number and hearing the automated message in the young female voice gave her a giggle. For a man who dealt with women all day, he certainly didn't know how to record an inviting message. One that would encourage someone to wait for a person to pick up the phone, and not hang up. "That's an easy fix; I'll offer to record one for him."

"Freddy," Sally said as he answered the phone. "I know you're busy, but I must stop by in the morning to go over a couple of things. And to get your signature so I can file your tax returns electronically."

"Sure. And, Sally, you are way overdue for a trim. I can't have anyone representing me looking like a shaggy dog."

"I could do with a trim, and how about a manicure and pedicure?"

"Finally, you are listening to me. Meet me at the shop at 9:30. You will be my first customer of the day and we can talk then."

Thinking about a full morning devoted to her personal care was a surprise. She had been trimming her own hair and not paying attention to her nails for months. *What's going on?* she wondered. *First wanting to see more of my family. Now thinking about my grooming… or lack of. Jeanne would say "at last." As if I hadn't been listening to her advice to get a life.* That brought a smile, and seeing her desk was all in order, headed for the kitchen and wine. *Hmm, has wine at the end of the day become a ritual?* Ignoring the thought, she poured her usual white wine.

The counter had been brightened by her mom's gift of a basket of Jersey farm grown tomatoes, the sweetest Sally had ever tasted. Picking one from the basket, she took out a cutting board and sliced it in several thick slices, then got some mozzarella from the fridge, sliced that, and arranged alternate white and rich red slices on a plate. A quick drizzle of homemade balsamic vinaigrette and a glass of wine, and she realized she hadn't prepared anything like this in months. She'd been cooking just the basics. *Basics for me, anyway*, as she thought about the soups or stews she'd cook on a Sunday and eat for most of the rest of the week.

A lovely tray mounted on an open kitchen shelf drew her attention, and reaching for it, placed glass, plate, napkins, and utensils on it and walked into her den-like area off the living room. Lifting her glass in a toast she said, "Sally ole girl, to you." Settling in for an evening of television, she finally relaxed with not a thought of anything serious to mar her peace.

* * *

Freddy's salon, Germaine Maison, was located on the ground floor of a six-story building that had one time been the family home of an earlier New Yorker. Situated in the east forties of Manhattan, it was a city block Sally only visited when coming to see Freddy. The entrance was old brick and once you entered the shop, you were in a modern glass and stainless-steel world.

"Good morning, Mrs. Scott," said Helena, Freddy's wife, manicurist, and receptionist.

"Hi, Helena. Today I am here as a customer. Your husband thinks I've been neglecting my grooming," Sally said with a wink. She liked the couple, both in their mid-forties, and attributed their shop's success to the personal attention they gave to everyone who entered their salon.

"Well, well, the hermit has left her cave," greeted Freddy with a hug. "Step over to my sink, and after a wash, I will begin to uncover that pretty young woman I first met."

"I am placing myself in your care, and the manicure and pedicure to that of Helena. I haven't thought of a treat like this in a very long time." As she settled in the chair in front of the sink, and felt Freddy enfold her in one of his waterproof capes, she closed her eyes. Sally couldn't remember when she had last enjoyed his scalp massage. Freddy's skill relaxed her like nothing except maybe a full body massage could.

"*Mm*, this is wonderful," Sally said as the water, not too hot or cold, began to flow over her head. "Freddy, you have magic fingers."

The escaping chuckle made her smile. "Sally Scott, you are a delight when the non-professional you shows up. I would love to see more of that woman. She is the kind of customer Germaine Maison is known to attract."

When her hair had been towel-dried, she moved over to Freddy's chair, positioned in the front of his shop. A place to watch over his staff, and to Sally's mind, show off his talent.

"As for your reputation, have you and Helena thought of expanding? Maybe a second location in another neighborhood. Say, Madison Park Green? That has become a new location for businesses seeking lower rents and new customers."

"A second location would cost money. We're comfortable. While the profits aren't what they once were, we're settled," Freddy said as he continued to snip away at her hair.

"I've been looking over your receipts. As to covering all your costs, you could rent out your chairs and increase profitability in a neighborhood with lower rents."

"I could never rent these chairs. My customers, while not visiting as often, would go somewhere else," he snapped.

"Well, think about it. Why not take a visit to the Flatiron area and check possible locations? It couldn't hurt. Maybe take a photo or two of possible buildings and check their rentals. Who knows, you could even visit several days each week to keep the Germaine Maison reputation intact."

Later, having reminded Freddy that without detailed customer tickets she couldn't keep track of his sales, and seeing his interest at her suggestion to prepare the tickets electronically, Sally was pleased with the entire morning. She'd work out a bookkeeping system easy enough for computer phobic Helena to use.

With hugs and kisses for her new look, Sally headed out the door, wondering where she should go next. "Shopping," she exclaimed. "Over on Fifth Avenue. I'll make a day of it."

Chapter 14

"Hey, Jeanne, are you doing anything right now? I know it's last minute, but I'm uptown and thought we could go to lunch. Maybe that little Italian restaurant Ryan introduced you to?" Sally's enthusiasm was evident in her voice.

"Is this my old friend, Sally Compton Scott, or am I being scammed?"

"It's me. I just left Freddy's, bought a too-expensive silk blouse at Saks, and decided lunch with my best friend would complete my day."

"Yes, to the restaurant, and yes to lunch. I'll make reservations for half an hour from now and text you the address. I'm hanging up before you change your mind."

The small restaurant was one Jeanne raved about. Sally wasn't sure it was the food, or having begun her infatuation with Ryan that colored her taste buds. It wasn't the décor, which was utilitarian. A place for business lunches between coworkers, not some place to wine and dine a client.

"Let me take a look," Jeanne said as she approached the front of the restaurant and began to walk around her friend. "Hair, a dress, heels? This is someone from my past and I couldn't be happier that she's returned."

Hugs and kisses, and the two walked into the restaurant.

"I don't know this restaurant, Jeanne. But you've mentioned it often," Sally said, following the waiter to a quiet table mid-way in the long narrow room.

"Well..." Jeanne began with a dreamy smile. "It was where Ryan took me the first time I called him to discuss you."

"Why in the world would you call Ryan, someone you only met at my wedding?" Sally asked, bemused.

"Ah, well, you see when you came back from Antarctica and were dealing with all that you had to, Tyler's death, your grief, and bills, I was worried sick. I just knew Ryan was the kind of man I could go to for advice."

"Advice? I was handling everything; what did you think he could do to help?"

"That's where fate came into things. You see, he loves you like a sister, and knew Tyler's secrets. But all he wanted to do was help you get through the funeral and settle Tyler's bills. Sally, did you know he was prepared to pay them if necessary?" Jeanne said as she reached out and took her best friend's hand. As she looked her straight in the eyes, she made the decision to be candid. "Honey, Ryan told me that Tyler was stretched so thin he was afraid they would foreclose on your house."

Tears began to seep from Sally's eyes. "He knew about our financial problems? Why didn't my husband share them with me?"

"Ryan wouldn't hurt you for the world. Anyway, we met a few times and each time I learned something else Tyler failed to share with you."

"Such as? Don't you dare keep anything from me," Sally ordered.

"That he was running as fast as he could to earn more money, and when Ryan suggested he cut back and you go back to work, Tyler snapped, 'No wife of mine is going to go to work because I can't afford to pay my bills.'"

It took Sally a few moments to review what she had learned after her husband's sudden death – that they were way over extended. On top of the bills they already had, Tyler went out and paid for their super expensive trip to Antarctica because he wanted to show her how much he loved her. "Yes. It's three years later and I've come to terms with my part in our financial mess. Jeanne, I'm to blame for Tyler always needing money."

"What? How can you be to blame?" Jeanne asked, confused.

"Because I kept talking about the family we were going to have. And, Jeanne, I wasn't listening to the fact that Tyler never shared in those dreams. He so wanted to make me happy that he kept silent and just worked harder."

Sally looked at her friend and knew she had more to share. "Jeanne? What else aren't you telling me?"

"Tyler didn't want any more children because he was afraid he couldn't earn enough to support Judy and Billy, let alone children you might have had," Jeanne explained.

Sinking back in her chair, Sally began fingering her fork, and knew this was the hardest thing Jeanne ever had to tell her. "Jeanne, I know. Did Ryan tell you that Tyler kept a diary of my fertile days and made sure he wasn't home? I never knew. Again, he was reacting to my dreams of a family of our own."

Shaking her head, Jeanne sat quietly.

"Well, what a downer this has turned out to be." Sally rallied and was pleased to see that her friend snapped out of her mood.

"Absolutely. We can't waste a new haircut and polished nails, not to mention having lunch in the middle of the week," Jeanne added.

As she raised her glass of water, Sally gave her new favorite toast. "To friends."

"To friends," Jeanne replied.

Chapter 15

Still smiling after her day of beauty and lunch with Jeanne, Sally entered her apartment, kicked off her heels, and headed for the kitchen. The ringing of her phone stopping her halfway there. "Now what? It's after four; my clients always call in the morning," she muttered as she answered the ringing phone.

"Mrs. Scott, this is Joe. Detective Logan is here and wondered if he could speak to you."

"Sure. Send him up."

Opening the front door, Sally was surprised by the huge grin on Detective Logan's face.

"This is a surprise," he said, delighted by the lovely vision before him. "Am I interrupting something?"

"Interrupting me… no, I just got home. I was about to make some tea. Would you like some?"

With Logan following her into the kitchen, Sally was aware that, while this was the first time he had been to her apartment, he wasn't looking around. He was looking at her. A slow blush began to spread. *Stop acting like a teenager.*

"How's the case going? Any leads to the possible killer?" she asked over her shoulder.

"Actually, I would like to go over a few things. Maybe something will trigger another area to follow up on."

Leading the gorgeous man to the dining room, with a tray of steaming mugs of tea, Sally was again surprised to be asked to help with this man's search for a killer.

"You know, I don't really know very much about you, Mrs. Scott," he began.

As she looked up into the kind blue eyes, she made a decision to relax and go with the conversation. Sharing her personal life wasn't something Sally did, especially since she moved into the city. Living in a building of two hundred apartments made her feel exposed and only safe when cosseted behind the door to the first home she had made for herself.

"I don't mean to pry, but you have been very helpful to me with this case, and…"

"No. It's alright. You have been most proper, and this incident has made me painfully aware of the evil in the world. I just never expected it to fall so close to my front door." Sincerity was easy with this man. He should get a better idea of who she was, especially as he made her feel valued as an observer.

"As you know, I'm a widow, my husband having died in an accident three years ago. I have since then returned to finish my degree in accounting, got my CPA, and now work for several small businesses as their accountant."

"That's interesting. You seem so matter-of-fact about your life. Surely there's more to it than that?" Detective Logan's comment was a surprise, as she never thought of her life in those terms. One works to pay for their life's needs and, if lucky enough, enjoys that work. All of which she did.

"I'm not sure what you mean, but I do have a family nearby." Sally was puzzled by this line of questioning. What else was there to life? Confusion was clearly visible on her calm face.

"Well, I know you jog three times a week and that the staff thinks very highly of you. They told me that not everyone greets them by name and treats them as individuals. That alone is a special kind of person."

Her smile was genuine. "They are all very nice to me and make me feel safe. When I first moved into this building it wasn't finished, so as one of very few new tenants, the staff just seemed to go out of their way to fix things that got broken, or pick up my mail if I had been away. And, for a single woman, always had a kind word, joke, and smile when they saw me." The tea was cooling, and she watched the man seem to relax.

"Nice seems to be a very rare ingredient in my line of work. However, I did want to ask a couple of questions concerning the case. I've met with Lisa's aunt, who is now her executor, and she has agreed to keep the apartment until we find her killer. But she didn't know what her niece was working on. Only that she told her it was dangerous and did not want her involved. So, we now think that this book she was writing is an exposé on something. But a thorough search of her apartment didn't turn up anything. Our tech guys reviewed a notebook, flash drive, and her computer, but nothing indicated investigation into any criminal enterprise. Certainly nothing pertaining to a manuscript."

"And you think I might have some idea where she hid her notes," Sally mused as she got up and pulled cookies from a ceramic jar on the kitchen counter. Returning with the plate in hand, she set it down and was pleased to see him reach for one.

"If I wanted to hide something that I worked on every day, I would keep all records on a flash drive and have it conveniently hidden nearby."

"We looked everywhere. Our computer technicians went over every inch of every piece of electronics we found."

"Did you check things like cereal boxes, coffee cans, boxes of soup?"

"Yes. What are you driving at, Sally?" His attention was riveted on her next words.

"When I set up my office, I consulted with my brother-in-law, who is an attorney, who also has CPA accreditation. He wanted to make sure that all my clients' files were safe from hackers. He knew I wasn't completely updated on computer security, other than having the appropriate software installed on my cell phone and desktop systems. He mentioned I could buy a replica of any household or kitchen item that had a false bottom in which I could, at the end of every day, or whenever I left the apartment, place my flash drives or memory cards. I just thought if I knew about something like this, and she was working on a dangerous story, she might do something similar."

When Detective Logan quickly rose and enfolded her in a deep hug, Sally's heart stopped. Pulling back to look up at his face wreathed in smiles, all she could do was smile back.

"I have to go," he said and, with another quick hug, left her to wonder what had just happened.

Chapter 16

Opening his cell phone, Jace's mind was busy with possible hiding places for Lisa Clark's notes. "John, grab Bill and meet me at Lisa Clark's apartment. I have some ideas of new places to search for that manuscript."

With the apartment having been closed up for two weeks, Jace was met with a wall of hot, stuffy air. Walking to the air conditioner, he turned it on and stood looking about the studio apartment. *I never thought of hiding anything in a can of coffee or cereal box. What ideas did the vic come up with to make sure her work was kept secret?*

"Come in, men, let's take another look and see what we may have missed," Jace began. "This time, Bill, check out every box or can in the kitchen cabinets, opened or not. Look for false bottoms, bulges where there shouldn't be any. John, did the guys check the laundry basket, in addition to her closets… underside of drawers… things like that?"

"Yeah, I saw them tear everything apart…" As John looked around the room, he noticed one thing that hadn't been checked. "You know, Jace, those curtains are hung on the thickest curtain rods I've ever seen. My wife just bought new drapes and when she asked me to go to the store for rods, the selection didn't include any like these. Maybe…"

As the two men walked to one of the two windows in the apartment, John, who stood over six feet, reached up and lifted the rod off its brackets. Unscrewing the finial at one end, he turned the rod on its end and saw a small flash drive fall to the floor.

"Good thinking," Jace said. "Let's check the other rod and the one in the shower. Try to think of another unusual place to hide things."

After an hour's search, where nothing else had turned up, Jace turned off the air conditioner. Then, after putting the apartment back together, gave it one more look and shook his head in resignation. "Let's go back to the office and see what this little bugger has to tell us."

* * *

With all three men scanning the contents on the flash drive on Jace's office computer, their questions increased. "Jace, it looks as if she was compiling resources explaining ways to hide money. She's listed a couple of well-known mystery writers, a few non-fiction titles, and library documents with dates going back almost a century," John said.

"The dress shop owner mentioned Clark was working on an exposé involving money laundering," Jace said.

"Yes. But this list is way too involved to lay it off on hidden bank accounts. She's also looking into topics involving the Italian Mob of the '20s," Bill exclaimed.

"Okay, next step. Each of you check out one or two of those library listings on the '20s and see if anything could be remotely connected to a modern-day crime. A person or persons unknown. A location used by criminals to hide cash. Something we can follow up on," Jace said. Sitting back, he thought of the videotapes he'd checked out the previous day. "Hey, guys, those tapes I looked at did prove interesting. Just as John said, the vic left her aunt's apartment the day before her death, but didn't leave the building. She took it to the fifteenth floor."

"I made a list of the residents and who owned or rented their units, just as you instructed," Bill said. Opening his notebook, he read the names of the residents on the fifteenth floor. "Oh, by the way, each unit on the fifteenth floor is owned by the resident, all except for Mrs. L. Raskin and an Aiden Raskin. They rent from Allied Realty."

"Okay, I'm going to follow up with Clark's publisher and her coworkers. Bill, check out that realty company, and John, see if the Raskin name appears on Google."

As Jace reviewed his notes, he became more interested in the vic as a journalist. "Well, young lady, I wish I'd met you alive. Your mind fascinates me. Money laundering, criminals, and searching through information going back a century. What a story that might make. I guess you were thinking the same thing."

Chapter 17

"Jeanne, surprise, I'm going shopping for new clothes. Do you want to join me at Megan's?" Sally announced in the early morning call. Sally knew it was her friend's day off and she had been urging her to get out of her sweats and back into what she called *Sally* clothes. Of course, Jeanne agreed.

Megan greeted them with open arms. "The world has just come to an end," Jeanne said, all smiles. When she followed up with, "This plain Jane wants to morph into a butterfly," making laughter spark all around.

"Cara," Megan called out, looking for her assistant. "Ah, here you are. I will need you to get our main dressing room set up. I'll hand you the garments, and we will have the fun of selecting Mrs. Scott's new look."

Three hours later, Sally was tired, but excited. She knew Megan was more than a shop owner; she knew how to bring out the best in each of her customers.

"Okay, Sally Scott, let's lay out your selections," Megan said. With Cara's arms loaded down, Megan lifted the garments one by one and arranged them on a rack. Tops hung with the appropriate slacks, suits with the correct blouse, and one addition, an all-weather coat that pulled each of the outfits together.

"Not a black item in the group," Jeanne said happily. "Now, Sally, which are you going to eliminate?"

Sally just sat there and looked at the collection. It was basic, but not boring. Where she would have chosen basic black, Megan had chosen navy or brown. Where she would have selected cotton for the tops, for easy care, Megan had selected either synthetic or silk. There wasn't an extraneous selection in the lot. She could see herself in each of the outfits as she visited her clients, instead of the clothes she continued to wear… all neat and tidy, but tired by comparison.

"Megan," a confident Sally started. "I'll take them all. And maybe when I get home, I'll retire my dreary looking suits that I've been wearing for the past three years." Sally was secretly relieved that not only could she afford the purchases, but was delighted to have made the decision. Spending money on herself was not something she did often.

"That calls for lunch on me. Megan, can you join us? There's a little place around the corner that looks cozy," Jeanne said.

"Ah, ladies, I wish I could, but I can't leave Cara alone. I'm expecting a shipment for the fall to winter seasons. I'm sending you off with my celebratory thanks for including me in Sally's coming out party. And Sally, I'll hem those pants and deliver everything to your apartment later this week."

* * *

Settled in Sally's living room, Jeanne looked around and noticed how sterile it was. The sofa she was sitting on didn't have a dent in any of the cushions. There weren't telltale signs like a book or magazine indicating that Sally even used this room.

"Girlfriend? What do you do when not working?" Jeanne began. "Read, watch TV, schedule a visit to the opera, or a museum?"

It had been a wonderful day, and Sally returned to the living room with a tray of Jeanne's favorite brownies and a pot of tea. She had been in a baking mood a few nights earlier, and loneliness sent her into the kitchen where she baked an old favorite of Tyler's. Setting the tray down on the coffee table, Sally thoughtfully answered her friend, knowing that she would be disappointed with her limited lifestyle. "A little television. Usually I put on a record; blues mostly. Why?"

"Well, now that you have the wardrobe, you should be going out more. Maybe take a trip. Don't your accounting clients have a pause after third-quarter taxes? That would give you a couple of weeks to visit some of those places you told me about."

"Oh, I couldn't travel by myself. Those were trips I was going to take with Tyler."

"You know that before I married my dream of a husband, I traveled. Off season, of course, it's less expensive and not as crowded."

"You always sent me postcards. Let me see, Venice, Paris, Bahamas."

"Yes, and each of those trips I took by myself. It forced me to meet new people and each time it made me think beyond my little world of the hospital and my apartment. It might be just the thing for you. Open your eyes to new cultures, colors, and people from someplace other than New York City."

"Why do you think that's important? I'm happily adjusting to the hustle and bustle."

"Travel has made me realize that this city is a microcosm of the world. You can order up dinner of any cuisine, at almost any price. Just sit in Central Park and you will hear languages from Asia, South American, even Australia. When you meet people from other cities, you find they talk about different things. I've found it fun."

"Like what different things?'

"Local happenings. Historic tales and architectural treasures. Unique expressions, differences in everyday fashions. Noted skills like lace making. Of course, my favorite activity… tasting delicious foods in each location. You're a foodie. You'd love it."

"I guess. Maybe later this year."

"I just think that we isolate ourselves in our homes. I find it very limiting."

"What are you suggesting, exactly?" Sally asked, not knowing what she was driving at. Jeanne was well traveled and curious. Something she apparently wasn't. Or was it that she had focused all her energies on life with Tyler?

"I think it's time you get out. Go to a play, matinee if you aren't comfortable going out in the evening. Check out the latest museum exhibits. Did you know we have a store front museum about firefighters, a museum devoted to math, even a museum of sex?"

"I know you're kidding, but you do have a point. I have enjoyed our lunches, and today was a gift. Fun and with a purpose, all in one. I promise to think about it. Happy?"

"Yes, and how could I be critical when you indulge me with brownies?"

Chapter 18

The morning looked bright, and since Sally had no appointments, she was planning on catching up on her billing. Opening the newspaper, she saw an article about a robbery on the upper westside of Manhattan. Apparently, someone had broken the windows of a phone store and stolen all the merchandise on display. So far, the police had blurry photos of the robbers captured on the store's video camera and were canvassing the neighborhood to see if anyone had seen something.

"Crime. I can't seem to get away from it," she mused, taking another sip of her morning coffee. Maybe Jeanne was right. Get out and see something other than my clients.

Opening her computer, she did a Google search for small museums. When the list came up, one museum jumped out at her. The Museum of the American Gangster. Reading the brief description, it said it was located in a speakeasy at St. Mark's Place, a neighborhood once frequented by Al Capone, Lucky Luciano, and John Gotti.

Still not familiar with the named streets, as all the streets and avenues she traveled on were numbered, she googled the address and found she could walk to it, giving her a reason to get out and enjoy what promised to be a delightful, sunny day.

"Perfect. If I'm involved with a murder victim, I might learn something from legendary criminals of the past." Sally knew she was being dramatic, but then finding a woman killed in her building was nothing if not traumatic.

* * *

Settling in for a quiet late afternoon and early dinner, Sally pulled out a pad and pen and began making notes of what she had learned in her tour of a townhouse with two addresses – 78 and 80 St. Mark's Place.

One building with divided front entrances, one to a home and the other a hidden speakeasy.

The main address was to a brownstone home that had been set up as a museum featuring displays of guns, photographs, and newspaper coverage of not only murders, but rum running during prohibition.

I've never really thought about crime as a business. Crimes she had read about in the newspapers displayed in cabinets and on the walls of the museum were all about extortion, rum running and speakeasys. About using guns and violence to maintain control over their various businesses. *I guess they are businesses. How naive of me.*

She wasn't all that ignorant. After all, the newspapers she read also reported on crime. The drug trade made huge sums. So did sex trafficking. Then, of course, there was extortion, and that probably existed in the days of the Roman Empire.

On closer study, Sally saw that the museum's exhibits highlighted how the Italian Mob used extortion to extract payments for protection or silence. Additionally, they ran rackets ensnaring local businesses, further drawing them into their web. Of all the schemes, rum running was the only crime no longer practiced when liquor sales became legal.

That required a fresh bottle of wine. As she headed for the cabinet, Sally decided that tonight she wanted to sip a glass, or two, of Malbec, a wine she only drank when she wanted something with more body.

Let me see, I do the books for businesses. For those who take cash, not just credit cards, they take the cash to the local bank where it is deposited in the business account. Since all my clients are legitimate, the bank has their financial information, and I use their statements when completing my records. Everything's above board and the government knows the true earnings as reported on their tax returns.

But the cash my clients take is never in the hundreds of thousands, or millions of dollars. What would I do with that amount of cash? In the old days, I could have hidden it in a safe, or opened a secret Swiss bank account. No longer.

I wonder if Detective Logan would give me a quick course in hiding money? Or, maybe my professor of business ethics might be willing to answer some questions.

Closing the pad, she turned on the television news and the story being broadcast was about cryptocurrency. "Ah. I think a trip to the library is in order."

Chapter 19

Friday and the last client she saw was Megan. It had been a quick stop to pick up her research on a possible new location for relocating her store, or opening a second smaller shop. Sally had reviewed Megan's proposal and offered some slight adjustments. And added her pros and cons for consideration.

"Hi, Scotty. Have a nice night," Sally said, on greeting the evening doorman. Heading for the elevators, she muttered, "I need a shower." Unlocking her front door, she quickly headed to her bedroom, and the promised relief from another hot, humid day in the city.

All snug in a fluffy robe and slippers, Sally walked into the kitchen, only to be drawn back to the living room by the ringing of her phone. "Sally Scott," she said somewhat distractedly.

"Mrs. Scott, it's Jace. Jace Logan."

Caught by surprise, as she hadn't spoken to him in a couple of weeks, all she could say was, "Hello."

"Look, I'm calling to see if I might take you out for a low-key bite. It would make the end of this week more pleasant than the rest of it has been."

"Ah, I don't know. Is that allowed? You know, because I'm a witness of sorts."

"The emphasis is on low-key."

"What time did you have in mind? I just settled in after a busy day myself."

"I can't finish up here until six-thirty. Would seven be alright? I can meet you at your building. It's a nice night for the short walk over to the river."

"Yes, Jace, I'm looking forward to it." Hanging up, she thought, *More questions*? *Maybe not?*

Sally looked in her closet and made a drastic decision, selecting one of her most feminine dresses. It was a bit upscale for a walk, but she could dress it down with a shawl. *I guess I'm dressing for that, maybe not.*

* * *

"Good evening, Mrs. Scott," Jace said, his face wreathed in smiles.

"Sally, please. I'm a bit overdressed, but I needed a pick me up and you came to my rescue," she replied. Jace's appreciative smile wasn't lost on her.

The short walk to the East River gave Sally time to ask Jace about her fascination with money laundering. She found, however, he kept changing the subject from the case and back to a walking tour of the neighborhood.

"I'm taking the long way around Gramercy Park. I didn't want you to miss those two buildings on the south side of the park, one being the home of Edwin Booth, brother of John Wilkes Booth, who assassinated President Abraham Lincoln."

"My own private tour guide." Sally laughed, enjoying Jace's smile.

"And now, Sally, it is the home of the Player's Club and in their library is a copy of the handwritten letter Edwin wrote to the people of America apologizing for his brother's actions." As he pointed to another wider brownstone, he told her it was the home of the National Arts Club, where members and their guests met regularly for lectures or to share a drink and dinner.

"I must take one of those neighborhood walking tours," Sally replied. "If I'm going to make my new life in a historic neighborhood, it's my responsibility to know more about it."

Once settled at an outdoor table by the river, Jace walked over to the food truck and placed their orders for tacos. Sally watched him bring their paper plates to the table and, seeing his occupied expression, knew he had something on his mind.

"You wanted to ask me something, Jace?"

"You mentioned your new life. I'm curious. I know people have stages in their lives, childhood, school, work, marriage. But it was the way you said it that has me curious."

That's unexpected, she thought. Pulling the wrap on her shoulders a little tighter, Sally wondered if she trusted this man enough to speak of personal issues. Widowhood, being top of that list. "New life for me began when I moved out of the house my husband and I shared into my apartment. I was twenty-nine and had never lived on my own. I went from my mother's house to an apartment I shared with my best friend, to life with my husband." She saw that Jace was following her every word. "I needed to earn a living, and navigate a life on my own." Looking away, she didn't know whether to continue. Then, on impulse, decided she wanted to share something she hadn't spoken about since Tyler's death. Jace was the first person outside her small circle who might understand. Clearing her throat, she added, "And to deal with the solitude and loneliness that haunts me still." She felt his large hand touch the back of hers and give it a gentle squeeze. Relieved that he did understand.

"That explains a lot. You see, people that live on their own either adjust to it and continue to follow their dreams, or they recede from the world."

"And which am I? I live and work from my apartment," Sally all but challenged.

"You are building a business, so you are not hiding. You are very well thought of by the building staff, so you are not a recluse. And your assistance with this murder investigation shows a curiosity that I expect will continue to add new avenues of interest to your life."

Surprised by his view of her life, one that she had never considered, Sally sat back and just smiled. "Do you conduct private sessions to help wandering souls find their true course in life?"

"I would if the client was you. Sally, this is a bit forward and certainly not professional. However, I am on my own time," Jace said, taking a sip of his drink.

Jace's soft, sexy voice certainly had her attention.

As he looked up and saw Sally's smile, he continued in a low, soft voice. "I find you not only attractive but interesting. And, I can't say that about many women I meet. And I would like to spend more time with you."

If looks could melt. While she had been flirting with the idea of allowing herself to begin a romantic relationship with Jace, she couldn't decide how to treat his comments that put his feelings out in the open.

"Jace, could we just enjoy this lovely mood and not mess it up?" As Jace sat back in his chair, she reached out for his hand, only to see confusion. "Jace, it isn't that I'm not interested. It's just a bit too soon." Seeing Jace nod in understanding, she quietly swore not to do anything to hurt him.

With dinner providing a needed distraction, Sally restarted the conversation. "Jace, I was wondering if you might explain how someone would hide large sums of money. I looked it up on the internet and got stuff about cryptocurrency, added value cards... whatever that is. But didn't you say that Lisa was researching something about money laundering?"

"Yes. We found a flash drive, but it only contained a listing of resources she was going to check out. Lisa was also interested in illegal operations that, if true, are reminiscent of the Italian Mob from the last century."

"Gangsters? Did you know that there is a museum of gangsters here in the city? Well, I visited it and it had guns, photos of gangsters, along with newspaper coverage of their crimes, and a hidden speakeasy with an escape route to another street. They were involved in murder, extortion, rum running. Things must have changed in a century," she said and laughed. "Jace, why are you looking at me like that?" she asked, reacting to his piercing gaze, as if he could read her mind.

"Look, Sally, please stay away from this investigation. I've already said too much. We can discuss anything in general, but I am begging you not to speak about this with anyone else." Jace squeezed her hand for emphasis.

"You're frightening me. It isn't as if I'm in any danger. All I did was report something on the floor of an elevator."

"Sally, we have to go. We can't talk about any of this. Discussing this with you could compromise the case. More importantly, you must promise me you will be careful."

Careful of what? she wondered. *He's making me feel that I have a target painted on my back.*

Thankfully, on the walk back to her building, Jace began to fill her in on the general topic of money laundering.

"So there are two aspects to the subject. If the money was somehow marked or counterfeit, a person might go to a casino and use it to purchase gambling chips. Then whatever they won would be considered legitimate, even when the casino reported it to the IRS. Or, they would take it to a bar and a cooperating owner would switch their clean money for the tainted bills, thereby widely distributing the fake currency, and in small amounts, not likely to be traced back to the bar."

He hadn't actually answered her question. "So where do you place the money to keep it hidden from the law? Especially huge sums?" She could feel the air change around him. It was as if a storm were brewing.

Jace took both of her shoulders firmly in his hands and turned her to face him. "Sally, stop, please. I've already said more than I should have, and most certainly can't answer that question. This case has gone from a local murder to something more." When Jace squeezed her shoulders a little harder and saw her wince, he quickly dropped his hands.

"Sally, please stay out of this for your own safety. I know you want to see Lisa's murderer caught and brought to justice, but it's bigger than that now. Don't let your curiosity get you into this any deeper than you already are."

"B-but..." she stammered.

"No buts. Too many people already know you found the body. The building staff, any number of your neighbors or friends. It only takes that wrong someone to overhear you discuss this and place you next on their hit list."

"I promise." Scared by the urgency of Jace's demand, Sally looked away from his unyielding stare. When she looked back up, his eyes were saying something entirely different from his hands. A disturbance of a different kind.

They had reached the entrance to her building and Sally took the easy way out by clasping his hand with a warm squeeze and giving him a heartfelt smile. A kiss would confirm her interest. She didn't have the courage. "Thank you for dinner. Good night, Jace."

"Good night, Sally," he said, as he turned and walked down the street.

Chapter 20

Jace's mind was focused on protecting someone who, for the very first time in ages, he felt personally responsible for. Sally was a potential threat to the murderer, but even more vulnerable because of her curiosity. During dinner, she came up with a theory that was pretty close to the reality of the crime. Lisa Clark's flash drive with her research list hinted at criminal ventures that Sally unknowingly equated to actions of the Mob from the last century.

Getting into his car for the hour-long drive to his home in Whitestone, Jace's thoughts turned to the few clues he had to this complicated case. The frustrating part of Lisa's file containing her research topics was that she hadn't left even a hint to the people she had been studying. So who in Sally's building felt threatened enough to kill in such a potentially public location? Sally said that they could have left the body in the elevator and pressed the button to the basement, where someone would be standing by to carry it to a waiting car. But her actions diverted the elevator before that could be accomplished.

"Shit. Double shit." The streets were busy with a solid flow of traffic, allowing his mind to wander. The vic's notes also hinted at forged documentation for persons or persons unknown. This was way out of his jurisdiction. He needed to talk to Tom and get a better handle on the potential scope of this case. An old friend, Tom Stone, entered the police academy with him five years before and was now with the FBI.

"Doesn't she know the danger she's in?" he shouted to the car up ahead, as if the force of his voice would somehow reach Sally. "The Mob, well, today's version, anyway."

Opening his cell phone, he punched the button for Tom's cell. "Don't you ever sleep?" he cussed as the call was answered on the other end.

"Jace? It's been ages. What's got you calling me at this hour?"

"If you are still at the office, could we meet over at our old haunt? That pub on third avenue?" Jace asked.

"Sure. And where else would a self-respecting agent be but at the office?" Tom joked.

"See you in fifteen." Hanging up, Jace turned the car back toward midtown.

* * *

Entering the darkened bar, he spotted Tom at a table in the back. As he passed the bartender, Jace ordered a scotch, and continued on his way. "You look old," Jace said, as he sat down opposite his old friend.

"You're not so youthful yourself," Tom answered. "What's this about?"

"I'm involved in a local murder that may be part of something much larger. If I submit my suspicions up the line, I lose control before I catch the murderer."

As the two men sat, heads all but touching, Jace was relieved when Tom agreed to back him up. Help him sort out whatever he discovered. "We have to keep this between us. At least until we know what we're dealing with," Jace said. "I certainly don't want to get you into any trouble, but until we know if it falls in your jurisdiction, we have to treat this as a local murder."

"Good idea. However, I think I need to speak to your witness," Tom replied. "Can you get her to meet at your precinct, but in a back office where we could avoid prying eyes?"

"Now? It's Friday night! I'm on my way home."

"Monday, first thing. Just let her know that I had heard she was exceptionally observant, and you asked me to speak to her. No need to get her frightened. Just say that I'd like to meet her," Tom said.

"What do you think you will learn? She's really an innocent in all this."

"Sometimes when a witness is faced with a stranger, they reveal an odd bit of information they hadn't thought important."

"And, knowing me, she is being more polite than digging back into her memory for something she previously hadn't considered," Jace said, completing Tom's thought.

"It looks like you are more than an uninterested party, pal. I have to see what this woman has to get your attention."

"Yea, maybe," Jace muttered, and taking a sip of his drink, wondered what Tom would think of Sally. "Monday. Is nine early enough for you?" Jace asked. Hearing a soft laugh, Jace relaxed. Tom was smart, and a good friend. His perspective went way beyond that of a local murder. Hopefully, together they would come up with new clues to who and why Lisa Clark was murdered. Jace had been getting hints from his captain that this case was taking far too long and should be placed on the back burner, threatening that if he didn't find something soon, he'd be reassigned to more current crimes.

"To Monday," Tom toasted and swallowed the balance of his drink.

"Thanks, pal. Till Monday at nine. I'll bring coffee," Jace said, and downed the rest of his scotch.

Chapter 21

It was the morning after her confusing dinner with Jace when Sally knew she was in trouble. How could she even be interested in another man when she still ached for Tyler?

I know. I'm going to make scrapbooks for the kids. Now where did I put Tyler's camera? It was Ryan's gift for their belated honeymoon trip to Antarctica. He said that he hoped Sally could make a scrapbook for his son and daughter, and of course she would make one for each of her stepchildren. As her plans took shape, tears began to seep and fall silently. Quickly brushing them away, she whispered to herself, "This won't do at all. It will be a gift from both of us."

Rummaging in the closet in which she stored the unpacked boxes from her previous home, Sally located the digital camera. Taking a quick look at the meter, she saw that there were about four hundred shots. "Well, that should give me enough for a nice album."

Just as she was about to head out to the hobby store for the materials she'd need, the phone rang. "Yes?" she answered without checking the number.

"Sally, it's Jace. I was talking to Tom Stone, an FBI friend, and he has asked to meet you. He's intrigued by your ability to observe some of the routines and residents of your building. We hoped you could meet us Monday morning at nine at the precinct."

"But, Jace, I told you the little I know."

"Yes. But would you do it for me? Maybe something new will crop up. Anyway, I think he just wants to meet the real deal."

Jace's light tone had her relax. "Sure. At nine, Monday. Anything else?"

"Not just now. Maybe we could catch up later next week. I really enjoyed last evening."

Be still, my heart, she thought. "I'd like that."

"Great. Bye, Sally. And thanks."

It took Sally a moment before she removed her hand from the phone. "Okay, I'm interested," she said, as if to confirm her suspicions. Then, looking at the list of scrapbook supplies, shook her head. Right now I'm honoring my husband. Dreams can wait.

* * *

Jace got to the office early and called Tom. "Tom, it's a go. Monday at 9," Jace said, wondering what Monday would reveal.

"Unfortunately, something's come up. It will have to be a video chat. Okay?" Tom asked.

"I'll set it up," Jace said, thinking that it might not scare Sally as much as Tom's intimidatingly severe approach to questioning a witness in person.

Next, he turned his attention to the research list from Lisa's flash drive. "Okay. First the Italian Mob file," he said. As he pulled up one newspaper article after another on his monitor, Jace thought about how much more colorful crime was in the thirties. Brutal, sure. By comparison, today's criminals he came across were slimy louts. While every New Yorker had seen the Hollywood version of real life, depicting the Italian Mob and their crimes, the library files reported on the five families that controlled New York City. One article led Jace to another, each one more interesting than the last. Of course, that was almost one hundred years ago. How did this relate to Lisa Clark's investigation?

Chapter 22

Sally had dressed in a conservative navy pantsuit and was waiting in the precinct lobby when a smiling Jace approached. "I love a woman who's on time." As he took her arm, giving it a little squeeze, he led her to the elevator. She knew he'd be there to protect her. Protect her from what, was the question? The worn elevator cab reminded her she was being questioned in a police station, not watching a movie.

"Sally, Tom is on assignment, so we arranged to have a videoconference. There is nothing to worry about; he just wants to ask a couple of questions. Alright?"

As she sat at a small table in front of a monitor, she nodded her agreement, wondering why the FBI wanted to question her.

"Tom Stone, this is Sally Compton Scott, the woman who spotted our murdered victim," Jace began, adjusting the camera and volume to more clearly hear Tom's reply.

"Mrs. Scott, it is a pleasure. Detective Logan has told me how kind and accommodating you have been. I just wanted to ask a few questions of my own. I wish it could be in person."

"Mr. Stone, before you start your questioning, can you tell me anything about the case? I feel responsible for finding that poor woman," Sally replied, trying to stay strong. All she knew was a woman was dead, what her name was, and that she had been researching a book. He looked nice, so maybe he'd tell her more than Jace had.

"Ah, curiosity," Tom replied in a friendly tone. "Mrs. Scott, this investigation is expanding into unknown territory. As you know, Detective Logan first began investigating a murder believed to be tied to a reporter working on a story involving money laundering. He contacted me when it became clear it may be more complex than that."

Sally knew by the limited answer it was all he was going to share.

"I wonder if you've seen anything out of the ordinary since Ms. Clark's body was found?" Stone asked, bringing the conversation back to the case.

"Not really. I work from home, so my daily comings and goings aren't on a regular schedule."

"But you do converse, or at least notice your neighbors?" Stone continued.

"If you mean has anyone new come to my attention? No. No one I haven't seen before."

"Has there been any change in those you do meet? Someone who might have stared at you, or whispered to a companion on passing you in the lobby?"

"Well, the day doorman has been extremely nice. However, there is a rule by management that prevents him from sharing information about other tenants or events like the police investigating a murder." She had tried to keep a defensive tone out of her reply and wasn't sure she had.

"Yes, the doorman, a Joe Franco. Have you spoken to any of your neighbors about the investigation?"

"Not really. I have talked to a couple of friends on different floors, asking if they knew of any residents that looked a bit strange." Thinking more about her neighbors, Sally said as an afterthought, "Did Detective Logan mention that, at first, I thought one of our tenants was kind of suspicious? Being curious, I went to one of his restaurants and noticed that while he looked like a Hollywood version of a producer, always seen with some gorgeous starlet, it was probably normal for him."

Whatever she just said seemed to make Tom Stone pause.

"Oh, there is another strange couple in the building, but they never speak to me." she continued.

"Why do you find them strange?" Tom asked in a matter-of-fact way.

"Well, I usually say hello to anyone I meet. But these two are like ice. Their usual response is a nod and then they quickly turn away."

"Strange?" Jace asked. "I don't remember you having mentioned anyone other than Maffeo, the restaurant owner."

"They just seem out of time and place. The old woman is dressed in a 1940s black dress with long sleeves and high collar and pearls. The younger man is tall, solidly built, also in a black suit, white shirt, and a strange tie clip. He may be a sort of companion. Anyway, his tie clip is at my eye level, so he must be over six foot two."

"Mrs. Scott, why did that tie clip catch your attention?"

Stone's curiosity surprised her. "Well, for one thing, even my well-dressed husband wore a simple gold bar of a clip. But this one, while gold, looked like some kind of symbol."

"Sally, could you draw it for us?" Jace asked, handing Sally a pen and pad. She thought about it and began to draw a hand with forefinger and pinky extended downward, and the thumb and middle two fingers folded back. "Something like this," she said, turning the paper toward the camera, then showing it to Jace.

"Tom, I recognize the symbol."

"Mrs. Scott, this is most helpful. Thank you for agreeing to talk with me."

As Sally started to rise, Tom Stone's voice stopped her. It was his hard tone, not the fact that he was still on camera. "Mrs. Scott, it is imperative that you not talk to any of your neighbors about this case. And when you leave your apartment, make sure you are aware of the personal space around you."

"Personal space? I don't understand." *That was certainly a strange thing to say*, she thought. Her nerves were once again on edge. As if being questioned by the FBI wasn't enough, now to be told to be on her guard?

"Sally, Tom is right. Your curiosity could draw unwanted attention. You must do as Tom says. And I am reminding you to leave things to us."

"Alright, Jace." Sally looked into his eyes, and had never seen them quite so hard. That scared her more than the FBI agent's warnings.

"Please understand, there may be people keeping an eye on you. Anything that seems unusual might raise an alarm," Tom explained.

"I don't understand. All I did was report that there was something on the floor of one of the building's elevators." Now she was unnerved. While Jace's questions had always sounded more like trying to solve a puzzle, Tom was ordering her to keep silent.

"Tom, I think we can let Mrs. Scott go. I'm sure if she thinks of anything, she'll get in touch with me."

"Of course, Jace. Thank you again, Mrs. Scott. You were most helpful."

Jace turned to Sally, and his frown was something she had never seen before.

"Tom and I are doing all we can to find Lisa Clark's murderer. Until then, you must stay out of this. Understand?"

As Sally left the precinct, her mind was a jumble of thoughts and increasing unease. Maybe it was nerves, but she had that prickling feeling at the base of her neck again. Remembering Jace's warning, she feared someone was following her. *But I don't know anything.*

* * *

"I'm looking at her now, Mr. Stone. She looks worried, lost in her own thoughts. That's when I saw a car pull away from the curb and follow her. I took some photos and am sending them now. I'll keep on the car and get back later."

"Thanks, Sam," Stone said, and switched his attention back to Jace. "Hey, when I asked to meet Mrs. Scott, I thought if your suspicions were correct, she may already be on someone's watch list. So I asked a friend to follow her when she left the precinct. Unfortunately, I was right. These photos prove it. I'll put a trace on the license and get back to you."

Jace sat quietly. Tom never whistled in the wind. When he suspected foul play, he began to send out feelers. The video proved that Sally was under watch by a person or persons unknown.

Unexpectedly, Tom's cell rang. "Jace, a minute," he said, closing down the microphone. "Yes, Sam?"

"I just lost the car that tailed Mrs. Scott somewhere around St. Mark's."

"Okay. Thanks. I'm back, Jace. That was Sam. He lost the car. Why don't I have him try to find it and then see where it goes? I'm betting he's going to find enough to get the FBI involved!"

"We ran background checks on every tenant in Mrs. Scott's building, but didn't find anything unusual. Maybe I should dig a little deeper?" Jace remarked.

"You might check out that odd pair. They may have some connection to one of the old Italian families. That tie clasp she drew for you is a symbol to ward off evil."

"I have an old contact who might catch us up on Mob etiquette," Jace said. And closing his phone, thought about Sally's latest revelations. *This is right out of a 1940s movie. Evil symbols? Where does that fit in today's world?*

Chapter 23

Sally's mind was lost in speculation about her meeting with the FBI agent Stone. Why would that tie clip be of interest?

I know what will take my mind off murder, finishing those scrapbooks. Once she'd changed into a pair of tights and loose t-shirt, Sally focused on sorting the photos on Tyler's camera. Having selected one hundred, she placed them on a flash drive. "I have to get a photo printer. But first to sketch a layout. The kids are going to love these," she said with delight. Each photo reminded her of those first couple of days on their trip. How gloriously happy they were. Tyler even adjusting to the forty-degree nights. She had felt somewhat guilty about suggesting they go to Antarctica when Tyler loved nothing more than golf at some sunny resort. But he quickly became immersed in photographing anything and everything. She smiled, remembering how happy he was bundled in his orange parka, oblivious to anything but his next shot.

Gosh, it's seven and I haven't even thought about dinner! Leaving her work on the dining room table, Sally went to the kitchen and pulled out a container of stew she had made a few days earlier. As it heated, she poured a glass of wine and settled in the living room to catch a late news program.

With dishes in the washer and the pot scrubbed, Sally poured a second glass of wine. What she needed was to sit quietly in the club chair, feet up on the ottoman, and close her eyes. Maybe she could shut out the present and bask in all things Tyler. "Shit!" she said, not happy to hear the ringing phone. "Hello?"

"Sally, it's Jace. I was wondering if you would like to join me for dinner on Saturday. Part of my personal introduction to another favorite New York spot of mine. Not business, I promise."

She hesitated, trying to balance her romantic thoughts of Tyler with her desire to get to know this man better. "Saturday would be lovely. Is this restaurant in the city? You have my curiosity piqued."

"No, I am taking you to the Bronx," he said, laughing. "It's time to learn that Manhattan is only one of five boroughs that make up this city. I'll pick you up at six. Will that be alright?"

"Should I dress in an explorer's outfit, complete with pith helmet?" she chortled.

"Just bring your lovely self, anyway you wish. See you then."

* * *

Conversation between them was so easy, Sally thought. "Are you always so interesting?" she asked as Jace pulled into a parking space before a restaurant with Dominick's written on the window. The entire hour and a half drive from Manhattan had been like chatting with an old friend.

She liked the way Jace took her arm and gave it a slight squeeze. Just as he had done at the precinct office. She could get used to this.

Seated at the table, Jace looked to her when he suggested they get a bottle of the house chianti. "Waiter, we will need a bit of time before we order." As the waiter poured each a glass of wine, he nodded and walked away.

"So where are we, exactly? It looks like one of those neighborhoods I've read about."

"Yes. It is, or was, predominantly Italian and is known for one of the great food markets where you could get anything a housewife needed to prepare meals for her family."

"Like the farmers' market on Union Square," Sally remarked.

"No. This is an indoor space where fruits and vegetables are stacked on counters like a colorful painting and people buy tomatoes, cucumbers, and peppers by the bushel. You see, in the '30s and '40s, women made their own tomato sauce, pickled cucumbers, and peppers. They didn't do takeout, or buy canned ingredients. Their pantries were well stocked with everything they needed to cook for their families."

"Not something my mom ever did," Sally said thoughtfully.

"After dinner, I'll take you by. I think you will understand the term neighborhood better."

Conversation continued about Italian families and customs as each local dish was served. Sally, of course, knew about spaghetti and meatballs, but had never heard of Pasta e fagioli, or Stracciatella, and each she tasted was a delightful surprise.

"Sally, I don't quite know how to say this, but I keep trying to find excuses to meet you. It isn't about the case, although your comments seem to provide new avenues to explore." He reached out to enfold her hand and, looking into her eyes, saw surprise instead of a smile. "After my comments at the river, you must have realized that I look forward to seeing you." His voice was low, obviously hoping not to scare her.

"Jace, I enjoy your company. Truly. The conversation is always interesting and you are so easy to be around. It's just I'm a widow and don't understand why I am so comfortable with you. I haven't dated since I met my husband. Now, I guess I think of myself as past any kind of romantic adventures." *Shit, did I say adventures?*

The smile on Jace's face was lit from within, and Sally could only admit to being drawn to it.

"Well, Sally Compton Scott, you are anything but past adventures. After all, I met you at the scene of a murder."

Chapter 24

Bleary-eyed, Jace had been at the precinct's computer for hours, researching several of the residents of Sally's building. The one that stood out for lack of background was Mrs. Lorenza Rafkin, owner of Rafkin and Sons, Antiquarian Books.

The store was purchased from a real estate firm in the late '30s. No specifics listed beyond the purchase price and address of the brownstone located on St. Mark's Place. "Wait a minute? Didn't the FBI agent follow that car to St. Mark's Square? Coincidence?"

Two hours later, Jace found that Mrs. Rafkin had married a Sargent Rafferty, back in the early '40s. He was a New York City policeman who died apprehending a shoplifter. Upon his death, she changed her name to Rafkin and opened the shop. She had one son. Guessing at ages, and working backward from today, if the woman was in her nineties, the son might be in his late sixties. So, who was the man that she was always seen with? Jace had at first thought he was a male companion, but now noted that he was also a Rafkin, living in a neighboring apartment. Could he be her grandson?

Digging a little deeper into the building's residential listings, Jace spotted another fact involving both Rafkins. As Bill noted, they didn't own their apartments. They were rented from the same company that Mrs. Rafkin purchased the bookstore building from. "This is interesting."

Maybe if he hadn't taken Sally to Arthur Avenue and introduced her to Italian family life, his mind would not be focused on Italian immigrants. Mrs. Rafkin married an Irishman, but had an Italian first name? And that tie clip to ward off evil… an old superstition.

Picking up the phone, Jace called Tom. "Thought you'd be interested in something I uncovered." After Jace filled him in on the interesting background of Mrs. Lorenza G. Rafkin, Tom said that he had instructed Sam to keep watch on the car and follow it wherever it went.

"Right, and I will continue to look into the Rafkin family," Jace added.

"I am hoping that Sam uncovers something we can officially work together on."

"Speaking of Sam, you might have him check foot traffic between St. Mark's Square, St. Mark's Place, and the streets in the area," Jace suggested and, hanging up, returned to the puzzle of the Rafkin family.

He had thought of calling it a day, but his initial research into Mrs. Lorenza G. Rafkin was murky, piquing his curiosity. Earlier in his career, Jace had gotten a New York Public Library card that gave him online access to the institution's private collections.

"Let's go see what I can find in antiquarian booksellers in the city." And so began what would become an education in this highly speculative market via trade publications, Auction House announcements, even the rare but occasional *New York Times* piece.

Exhausted, he turned off his computer, took his notepad and, placing it in his pocket, headed home. The big question: how in the hell did money laundering enter into the sale of old books and maps?

Chapter 25

With the bedspread crisp and in place, her bedroom was once again in order, reminding Sally that her mind may be messy, but she couldn't live in disorderly surroundings.

Work done for the week, check. Jeanne and Ryan expecting me for dinner a week from Sunday, check. That leaves this Thursday and Friday with nothing to look forward to. Is that what my life has become? Opening her computer, Sally scanned hotels within easy commute and one of the first that came up was Mohonk Mountain House and Spa. A spa? Why not? A couple of days in the peaceful Hudson Valley, away from honking horns and sirens, with every need from sleep and dining to healing spa treatments readily available. Reading the hotel's website, she realized that not only would she be escaping her limited life, but would be visiting a historic hotel dating back to 1869, when the founding family purchased 40,000 acres of pristine forested land.

There is a first time for everything, old girl. With that decided, she booked a room, rented a car, and began writing out a packing list of things to take for the short trip. For a moment, she remembered packing for overnight getaways with Tyler. *Stop it. Just stop it. It's my turn.*

* * *

The drive up to New Paltz eased Sally's mind. For once, she stopped reviewing her to-do list and simply enjoyed the soft music on the radio, along with the changing scenery. She kept to the speed limit. No rushing. No thoughts of work. And began to hum along with the radio.

Pulling up to the main entrance of an exceedingly massive Victorian building, she was amazed that she hadn't factored the size needed to provide all the hotel services listed on its website. They offered everything from seasonal fishing, horseback riding, to peace and quiet for those seeking relaxation.

Sally had splurged and booked a room with a balcony, and once unpacked, sat in a balcony chair, simply enjoying the view. The mountain foliage and variety of trees had begun to tint red and orange that would intensify as fall approached. *I'm going to order room service and just absorb this peaceful view.*

* * *

It was the second and last afternoon and Sally was enjoying a hot rock massage at the spa. She had sampled a meditation session and a yoga class, and realized she needed to include regular exercise classes in her daily schedule. Jogging was fine but definitely hadn't stretched her muscles stiffened by sitting long hours over her computer, and certainly hadn't freed her mind like the meditation class had done.

"*Mm,*" Sally murmured as the woman finished her hour-long massage. "You are a magician," she said as she slipped the young woman a healthy tip.

Tonight, you are dressing for a full restaurant experience. Cocktail at the bar, then full three course dinner in the dining room… a celebration of my new freedom.

* * *

It was four on Saturday afternoon by the time Sally returned the car. For some reason, she felt eyes on her back. Probably just the closeness of city crowds, she decided, and continued on her way home. Depositing her mail on the kitchen counter, she headed for the bedroom to unpack.

"What the fuck?" she cried at the ringing of the phone. "I haven't been home ten minutes."

"Yes?"

"Sally, where have you been? I've been worried sick," Jace said, the urgency of his tone causing her to frown.

"What are you talking about, Jace? I decided to take a couple of days away from the city and just got back." She could hear his breathing slow. "Why have you been trying to reach me?"

"Sally, I hope you enjoyed your two days. Let me take you to the park, we can grab a bite, and you can tell me all about it."

She didn't know what to say. Of course she wanted to see him. He was certainly on her mind and she realized it wasn't the murder investigation; it was that he had rekindled her emotions. She hadn't felt anything in three years.

"Sally, don't you want to see me?" a hesitant Jace asked at her silence.

"Oh sorry. Yes, Jace, I would love to see you. How about seven? I need some time to go through some business stuff first."

"Seven it is. Sally, I am really looking forward to seeing you."

Yup, she found Jace fascinating.

Chapter 26

With arms linked, as they headed toward Madison Square Park, Sally felt at peace. During her meditation session, she realized Tyler would always be her first love, and that didn't have to keep her from finding love again. Jace was stimulating, sexy, and thought she was intelligent, so who wouldn't fall for a man like that.

With hotdogs and coffee collected from the take-away food stall, Jace found a table away from the main area. "Let's settle here. I think this will be more private, away from noisy diners." Lifting his coffee, Jace said, "A toast. To your safe return."

Sally clicked her cup with his, but wondered at the wording of the toast. "Safe return? I don't understand."

If looks could convince her that there was something Jace wasn't telling her, his shifting weight as he looked down at his food confirmed it. "Okay, out with it."

"First, tell me about why you took your trip."

That was fair. She needed to become more open with this man if there was any hope of a romance. "I have been sequestered in my apartment for three years. I've accomplished all I had wanted from finding and furnishing the very first home of my own, to building a business with clients I enjoy. But when I looked at my schedule earlier this week, I had two days with nothing on it. Not even to clear out a closet."

"You schedule house chores?" She saw Jace smiling and felt comfortable enough to share a bit more.

"Well anyway, I thought that was very sad and decided to take a trip someplace."

"For the past three years, you've never ventured far from your building?"

She could see by Jace's puzzled expression he really didn't know her at all. "You are looking at someone who is only beginning to live her own life. And when I looked up places near the city and saw Mohonk Mountain House and Spa, it looked like just what I needed." Sally paused; she wasn't sure just how much to share. Jace seemed to be following her every word.

"And it was magical. I was pampered, soothed both physically and mentally, and it made me realize I was a new Sally Compton Scott. And I have to find out who she is."

"I must say I'm surprised. Your world is much smaller than I would have expected. But also looking at you tonight, you seem younger, fresher, and somehow more relaxed."

"Is there a compliment in there?" Sally said with a chuckle.

"Damn straight, young lady."

As Jace asked one question after another about her two days away, Sally couldn't remember anyone being as interested in what she did, or about her feelings.

"Okay, dinner eaten. It's your turn. Why were you so anxious about my not being home when you called?"

"I called your cell a couple of times, and when you didn't answer, called your landline and left several messages. But when I didn't hear from you, I worried that something had happened."

"My clients knew I was going to be away, my mom and Ryan and Jeannie also knew. And frankly, there wasn't anyone else in my world I expected to hear from. So, while I took my cell phone, I never turned it on."

"I don't know anyone who turns off their phone. Me, because of my job, and others who seem to have their phones glued to their hands. You, young lady, are full of surprises."

"Jace, why aren't you answering my question?" Sally asked more firmly.

"The case has gotten more complicated. I didn't want to tell you this, but when you left the precinct, you were followed by a man in a car. When Tom learned about it, he had his agent follow the man, only to lose him. It made me crazy when I couldn't find you."

"Are you watching me? Why? I don't know anything."

"I didn't want to say anything earlier because I didn't want you frightened and have you acting differently. Yes, we believe, and now know, people are interested in where you go and who you see."

"And knowing this, I'm just to pretend life is going along normally?" Sally cried out. "How am I supposed to do that, Jace?" she snapped and got up from her chair. "I think I'd like to go now." Jace knew not to say anything, placed an arm over her shoulders, and walked back to her building. Not a word spoken.

Chapter 27

"Tom, I just left Sally Scott, and she's safe. She decided to take a couple of days at a spa. But I had to tell her she was being followed, and that we were keeping an eye on her. I hated to do that. Now she's going to be wary and that may put someone on alert."

"Okay, we've been watching the car my agent photographed. It was parked on a nearby street. Yesterday, he took an early morning trip out to a service station in Bayville, Long Island, where he met up with a small pickup truck at a gas stop. The agent said at first he didn't think anything of it as the truck was pretty beaten up and driven by a shabby old man. But when the car approached the truck, another man got out and walked to our suspect's car, opened the passenger door, and got in. The old man got out of the truck, walked to the driver's side window, and had a brief chat with the driver of the car. My guy said nothing more transpired, just that the old man got back into the truck. By the time the car returned to the city, it was 3 a.m. and the street was dark. He lost the two men somewhere around the entrance to a butcher shop. But he sent me photos."

"Wait a minute. This is the block south of St. Mark's Place?"

"Yes."

"If my memory is right, and I will confirm later when I get to the office, that street is full of tunnels the Mob used during prohibition. We may have a connection to the 1920s Mob in New York."

"You follow up on that, and I'll see if we can locate the owner of the pickup."

* * *

Jace had been in the records department since it opened and searching the blueprints of buildings on St. Marks Place, but couldn't find any with the tunnels under the butcher shop. There was one man who might know, and he decided to pay him a visit.

Arriving at the retirement home, he asked to see Riccardo Bianchi, an elderly ex-seaman.

"Ricky, it's been a long time," Jace said as he gave the ninety-year-old man a hug.

"Si. Life is good? Catching all those old crooks?" Ricky said with a broad smile.

"Not all old these days. And not nearly as smart."

Jace led the wiry old man to the coffee shop and ordered two espressos. Pulling out a small flask, he raised it for approval.

"Nectar of the gods. Si."

This was the man who had led him to his first bust along the waterfront. When the case had been prosecuted, Jace made sure Ricky was safe, settling him into the seamen's retirement home. He truly enjoyed Ricky's company and kept in touch. At first, he visited just for coffee. And gradually stayed longer to hear the seaman's stories of his days in the Mob.

"How good is your memory, Ricky?"

"Better with another bit of sambuco in my cup." The grin was infectious.

"Are you sure your doctor won't kick me out?" Jace's question was partially in jest. This man was living with aches and pains earned as a young man. Either a cargo load hit his foot or some thug beat him for disrespecting some obscure Mob rule like being seen fraternizing with the wrong cop.

"Ricky, do you know the buildings on St. Mark's Place? Maybe who owned the one with the butcher shop on the next street?"

"That takes me back to my twenties. When I was good looking."

Jace waited. When Ricky told his stories, it took a bit before he had all the pieces in place.

"It wasn't just that butcher shop. It was the tunnels under it to two brownstones on St. Mark's. One was owned by a real estate company. A front for Gambino. The other was a speakeasy."

"And the tunnels? Why aren't they in the building plans in the city files?"

"*Stupidese*. They were dug to let the Mob meet privately, and speakeasy patrons escape during police raids."

"And rum running?"

Ricky looked Jace squarely in the eyes. "You aren't interested in the '20s."

"No, but your history has an interesting twist." Grabbing the man's hand, he placed a $100 bill in it, along with the flask of liquor, and squeezed it closed. "Stay safe. I may want you to meet someone special."

"You got a lady friend at last?"

"I finally listened to you. Didn't you tell me that I'd made my bones, but I'd never be a man until I loved a good woman?"

Jace really liked the old seaman. Their conversations reminded him of those he had with his father so many years ago. He too worked on the docks, but as a policeman, and drilled into his son's head the who and how the Mob worked. *Thanks Dad.*

Chapter 28

Sleep just wouldn't come. Not fighting it any longer, Sally got up and went to the kitchen and made a cup of tea. Settled in her favorite club chair, gazing sightlessly at the glorious view of uptown Manhattan in its evening glow, she couldn't figure out what had happened.

I'm living a good and safe life. The trip reminded me I have more ahead than those few years with Tyler. So what's the problem?

How in the hell did I get in the middle of a murder investigation with people following me? Is Jace right, and I'm at risk?

"This is no longer a puzzle that needs to be solved. It's my life," she swore. "I need advice from the only sane person with a brain I know, Ryan."

* * *

As soon as Sally entered Ryan's midtown office, he rushed to enfold her in a deep hug. She saw him study her expression, seeking a clue to the reason for her visit. By this time, Ryan knew not only everything about Sally Compton Scott, but how to read her.

Settled off to the side of the large office, Ryan poured a fresh cup of tea. "Ah, you knew I was in trouble," Sally said, relieved she didn't have to make five minutes of excuses for this impromptu visit. "I need advice and didn't want to worry Jeanne. Some rational thinking about the situation I seem to have gotten myself into."

"The murder?" Ryan said matter-of-factly. "I had hoped you would ask me for help. Why not fill me in?"

Her tears started, and Ryan was right there with a box of tissues. "You know the basics. My actions led to the discovery of a murdered young woman. Now I understand I am under surveillance by the local police and maybe the FBI... and people unknown."

"That's the summary. How about a few details? I'm an attorney. I need specifics," Ryan said in an off-hand manner.

His attempt to lighten the mood failed. Sally just nodded.

"I've been seeing Detective Jace Logan. At first, because it was me having spotted something in the building elevator and reported it to the doorman, who contacted the police when he saw the young woman lying on the elevator floor."

"Is this the young man Jeanne has mentioned?"

Why wasn't she surprised that Ryan knew about Jace? It reminded her that Jeanne was now family. Married to her brother-in-law and was therefore doubly protective of Sally. "Yes. The few meetings to answer some of his questions about our building... the residents, how the building worked... stuff like that. Well, they've become a bit more personal." Looking for disapproval from the brother of her former husband, all she saw was warmth, not criticism.

"Details? Sally, I think I have the players in this drama. What I want to know is why you feel you are under surveillance? Surely this detective doesn't suspect you of killing this woman?"

"Nothing like that. But earlier this week, he asked me to meet him at the precinct, saying that someone from the FBI wanted to talk to me." She could now see concern on Ryan's normally unruffled face. "They didn't ask anything special or different and I left the office. And…apparently, according to Jace, I was followed."

"Followed? By the FBI to keep you safe?"

"Yes, and someone else. Anyway, when I came back from my quick spa visit, Jace called and was really upset that I hadn't returned any of his calls to either my cell or home phone."

"We knew where you were. You never take your phone, or if you do, hardly ever turn it on." Ryan's matter-of-fact response helped her calm down. She wasn't the one at fault. Something sinister was going on behind her back.

"Ryan, I really do not know what the murder is all about. Just that Lisa Clark was working on an exposé about money laundering. Jace said he was prevented from sharing anything more. But if the FBI is involved, doesn't that make it more?"

She could see the wheels in Ryan's head turning. "What happened after you spoke to Jace and assured him you had just taken a couple of days out of town?"

"Well, I agreed to meet him later for dinner. And at dinner he told me about my being followed. That he hadn't wanted to alarm me, but didn't want me to act any differently, as he was sure someone in the building was keeping a close watch on my movements."

"Murder in your building, and the murderer is either a resident, or hired the killer. Yes, that makes sense," Ryan said, in full attorney mode.

"What do I do? I've been going blithely about my daily routine, never looking over my shoulder. But lately, and this may sound crazy, but sometimes when I'm out, I get a prickly feeling of being watched. Now with Jace confirming it, I don't know what to do. I can't stay cooped up at home. I've got a life. Work, a home, family. I feel I've been thrown to the wolves."

"Here, sip your tea. Then give me this detective's phone number. Maybe I can get a bit more information. Until then, you stay calm. Enjoy your new life. Okay?"

"Yes, Ryan," Sally replied, somewhat like a child to a parent. With a chuckle, she relaxed. Ryan would help her, just like he picked up the pieces when Tyler died.

Chapter 29

"Detective Jace Logan, please," Ryan said to the telephone receptionist at Sally's local police precinct.

"May I say who's calling?" she responded.

"Yes. Tell Detective Logan it's Sally Scott's brother-in-law."

Ryan was surprised at the speed with which he'd been transferred. "Mr. Scott," Jace said.

"Thank you for taking my call, Detective Logan. I was hoping that we might meet, say today after work? Sally is very precious to the family and I would like to help her in any way I can. She tells me that you have been meeting and while she knows a bit about the murder of that unfortunate young woman, she is still stressed and nervous."

"If you can come to the precinct at five today, we can talk. I'm not sure how much I can share, but I do owe Mrs. Scott for the help she has provided."

* * *

Being directed to an office upstairs, Ryan was met at the elevator by a man in his late thirties.

"Mr. Scott, thank you for coming."

Ryan was quick to size up the well-built man who had greeted him. There was a warmth he hadn't expected. What he'd thought he'd be meeting was a hardened crime fighter like those on television dramas. This man was a serious-looking professional who was giving him all of his attention.

"I don't mean to get in your way, Detective, but I would like to understand the position Sally is in and if she is in any danger."

"Mr. Scott, I must say I'm surprised by your call. And, having spent time with Mrs. Scott, I can understand your concern."

Once settled in a small room with space enough for a table and a couple of chairs, Ryan sat waiting. The room showed wear with paint peeling in patches, and the table stained with rings from wet coffee mugs. But this wasn't a lawyer deposing a witness and looking for clues to build a case; he was here to help Sally.

"Detective, can you tell me why Sally is still of interest? Surely she isn't a suspect?" Ryan was surprised by the young man's smile. Another mark in the man's favor.

"Mr. Scott, Sally is most definitely not a suspect. Has she told you how she became involved in the first place?"

Ryan nodded. "But after she reported what she saw, or thought she saw, I would think that would be the end of it."

The direct look he gave Ryan was serious. A no-nonsense expression that demanded attention. "Mr. Scott, your sister-in-law led us to identifying the victim in a matter of hours. Not days, as would be usual for someone found without any identification."

"Detective, please call me Ryan, and tell me why and how she seems to be a central source? Sally is one of the most honest and decent people I've ever known. I doubt she's come across anyone evil enough to kill."

Ryan watched as the man sat silently, staring at him as if to decide just what to answer. "Should she be worried?" he asked, breaking into the detective's thoughts.

"Simply, yes. While I have told her to be careful, that she is being watched by persons unknown, I'd rather she didn't know how serious these people may be."

"I really need you to explain so I can protect her."

"First, let me say I can't seem to get over Sally's genuine awareness of things around her. Like noticing the color of the fabric on the elevator floor and connecting it to a coat she saw at her client's shop. I personally visited the shop and when I showed the owner a picture of the victim, she not only gave me her name and occupation, but a place to start investigating her murder."

Ryan saw more than appreciation in the detective's view of Sally. He thought he saw admiration, and something more.

"Do you live in an apartment building in the city, Ryan?"

"No, a brownstone uptown. Why?"

"Well, if this murder were in a suburban community, we would be canvassing neighbors for information. In a high-rise building, you live in a contained neighborhood. Even if you don't know everyone, and that's hard to do in a building of two hundred apartments. But as you go about your life, you pass neighbors. Sally not only knows more about who lives in her community, but what goes on in it. Hence, her observations continue to give us clues to who might provide us with information about the murder."

"Are they still in her building? If so, I can get her to move in with me."

"We believe they are still in the building, but if Sally leaves, and isn't seen going about her normal life, they may get spooked. We can't have that since we are closing in on possible suspects."

"Spooked enough to go after Sally?" The flatness of Ryan's comment got Jace's attention.

"Yes. They have already killed once. One more wouldn't be a problem."

"Okay, she can't move. Could I have someone move in with her?"

"We are watching her. I told her as much the other night. I know she's scared. I thought she'd be more comfortable knowing. I guess not, since she came to you."

This wasn't what Ryan had expected at all. He hoped Sally was well out of the case. "So my sister-in-law is in the midst of an ongoing murder investigation." The look he gave the detective was anything but soft.

"Since you are close, maybe you could do me a favor, Mr.... Ryan?" Jace's change in tone sounded hopeful.

"I can, if it will keep Sally safe."

"Both I think," Jace replied. "My idea is to have people in her building think we have become a romantic item. Of course, if this were true, it would jeopardize the case. But think of it as an undercover operation. That would allow me to visit her on almost a daily basis."

"What aren't you telling me, Detective?"

"Well, I'm no prince. But your sister-in-law continues to fascinate me. In an unofficial way."

The strong man had whispered his request as if he was afraid to admit he was in love. Ryan couldn't have been more pleased. He liked this man for his straight forwardness, and the way he referred to Sally. She was due for a romance. This time with someone who would take care of her. "And how do you propose to tell my sister-in-law it's just to keep her safe?" Ryan said as seriously as he could.

"Ah, well. She knows we are meeting?" Seeing Ryan nod in confirmation, he continued. "Well, maybe you might tell her it was your idea? You know, then she'd go along with it and feel safe at the same time."

Holding out his hand to the hesitant detective, Ryan gave it a firm shake. "Absolutely, Jace." The air around the two men seemed to have calmed. Sally would be safe, though Ryan was betting Jace wasn't going to be.

Chapter 30

"Sally, how about coming over for dinner? Jeanne is cooking. She said you'd be surprised as it's not a frozen dinner." The laughter Ryan heard was reassuring. It was going to be some evening. He'd arranged for a babysitter to take the kids to a playdate. They'd be home by eight, which should give them time to hatch the plot he and Jace had discussed.

* * *

"Sally, here's a sidecar. Jeanne said it was a family drink." Ryan gave her a quick kiss on the cheek. "Let me take your things; Jeanne is in the den."

"Hey, girlfriend," Jeanne greeted as she rushed to envelop Sally in a hug. "I've made your famous spinach dip, and there is an assortment of cheeses to nibble on."

"You're cooking? And Ryan and the kids are still alive. What a lovely surprise." Sally's comments sparked laughter all around.

"Well, I'm not in your league with all those special recipes you cooked for Tyler. But, yes, I can cook," Jeanne said with a self-satisfied smile.

Ryan watched as Jeanne led the discussion, asking about Sally's clients. But he also noticed Sally's humor fade, and she began to twist her glass instead of sipping her drink.

"Okay, you two. What's up? You know you can't keep a secret, Jeanne."

"Here, let me freshen your drink," Ryan began as he picked up the cocktail shaker, not yet able to look her directly in the eye. "Actually, I think I have some good news. At least I hope so," he began as he settled in the chair opposite Sally.

"Good news? Is this about your chat with Jace Logan? I assume you two have spoken." She wasn't angry. After all, she asked Ryan to get involved.

"I really like him. We met and came up with an idea that you might think contrived, but it would keep you safe and maybe help you relax until this murder is solved."

"I'm waiting. When two men hatch a plot, it could only involve sex." It was one of her sarcastic comebacks when she wanted to change the tone of a conversation.

"Sex? You're kidding!" Ryan was completely offended that she would think he'd do anything like that.

"Ryan, it's a joke. Lighten up and tell me what you two decided."

"Sorry. Anyway, if Jace Logan were to be seeing you socially, it would make his frequent visits and being seen with you seem normal, not connected with the investigation. All the while, he'd be keeping you safe."

"Sally? Why the smile?" Jeanne asked.

"And this was Detective Logan's idea?" Her smile grew a bit wider.

"Yes. But as he explained it, it made sense. If someone in your building is watching you, they already know you two have spoken. This would hopefully make them think this was something other than part of the investigation."

"By the way, Sally, how often have you seen him? Considering you aren't a suspect…" Jeanne asked.

Ignoring her friend's subtle hint that there may be a romance brewing, Sally was curious. "And how often would I be seeing him?"

"Almost daily. The times of day would change. Maybe one day for lunch, another for dinner, and joining you for a morning jog."

"I can do that," Sally replied, her thoughts turning to something else. "At least it would take me from being the building widow to building chippie rather quickly."

"Sally, you aren't angry that I agreed to this plan?" Ryan asked, concerned that she had only asked him to speak to Detective Logan, not arrange a setup. He knew she hadn't seen anyone since his brother's untimely death.

It took a while for Sally to decide how to answer them. Obviously, they were concerned for her safety. But should she share her growing personal interest in Jace Logan? "Ah, no Ryan, I'm not angry. Actually, since I've seen him several times after work, anyone interested will already know that. Usually, a detective doesn't take a witness out to dinner." Looking up at Jeanne, she smiled. "Yes, he is an interesting man. I'd like to get to know him better. So, Ryan, I guess I should thank you." With a broad grin, Sally lifted her drink to say in toast, "Here's to my new best friend." Laughter followed, and she saw that Ryan was pleased.

Chapter 31

"Good morning, Sally," Jace said, greeting her at the entrance of her building. "Ready to show me how to get healthy?"

It was just past 6 a.m. and the first day of her new arrangement with Jace. She would find out if their jog could become a three-times-a-week routine, or if having him along would slow her down.

"A warning… I usually devote half an hour, then it's back to work. Ready?"

Talk had been intermittent and all about fitness. As they jogged around Gramercy Park for the last time, Sally finally admitted that she was interested in this man. *Yeah, once I'm out of some murderer's crosshairs.*

"Surprised myself," Jace said as he jogged up to the entrance of Sally's building.

"And me. You're pretty fit, Detective. Do you work out? I believe you said rarely. Well, the joke's on me," and with a quick hug left him at the entrance.

Waiting by the elevators to take her upstairs, Sally saw the Rafkins exiting. Not a nod of recognition, or a word spoken, as she watched them walk arm in arm out of the building. "I wonder if Jace is still outside. Or if he has spoken to those two," she muttered.

The apartment phone was ringing as she entered and, rushing to answer, was surprised to find it was Jace. "Sally, the two who just left your building. An older woman in black and a younger man. They just got into a black limo, with a uniformed driver."

"That is Mrs. Rafkin and her companion. They are always together."

"Can you tell me anything more about them? Bill did interview them briefly, along with the rest of the building's residents. But it was more along the lines of: did they know the victim; where were they earlier that day? That sort of thing."

"Abrupt. Not friendly. Seem to keep a regular routine. Nothing else really… oh yes, the man was the one with that strange tie clip that I drew for your FBI colleague."

"Great, and thanks. How about an early dinner, say five at that diner you like? I am afraid the department can only spring for the occasional restaurant meal."

"I'd love that."

* * *

Later, Sally felt more comfortable meeting Jace in the building lobby than his picking her up at her door. *At least for the present*, she thought.

"Dressed down, have we?" Jace said as he met Sally by the doorman's station.

"This is my normal attire – slacks and sweater or t-shirt. The woman you previously saw was a scared witness who thought she should look as professional as possible when dealing with the police." Her comment, delivered with a smile, was more of a tease.

"Ah, my favorite look, relaxed. So you won't fight me off at the end of the evening," he joked.

"I think I'm going to like this new arrangement. I love your flights of fancy."

With dinner ordered, Sally couldn't contain herself. "Okay, out with it. What about my neighbor's tie clip had you and the FBI so interested?" She watched as Jace sipped his coffee. It seemed he was never far from a cup.

"It reminded me that you are not yet a New Yorker," he said with a smile. "Those of us raised in predominantly immigrant communities learn a language of cultural symbols, along with a few swear words. That particular design is an Italian lucky charm of sorts, meant to ward off the evil eye. It is really old school superstition, but in the case of your two neighbors, signifies that they may have immigrant Italian family connections. So we, actually me, have been looking into the Rafkin family and its business dealings."

"Are they criminals?" If she wasn't frightened before, this certainly didn't calm her nerves. "Look, Jace, all I know about the Mob is what I've seen in the movies. Wiseguys, extortion, murder, and rum running. This is the twenty-first century; surely that old woman isn't a Mobster."

"Well, so far, my research has found nothing to think she is."

"But you are going to keep digging, because….?"

"Because, do you know of any man in his late forties who is so devoted to an old woman? According to you, they're always seen together."

"Point taken." Sally would let Jace worry about the eccentric pair. She was dealing with emotions she hadn't felt in three years.

Chapter 32

Jace, having left Sally at her building, rushed to FBI headquarters for a meeting with Tom, knowing that, like himself, Tom was always on duty. Calling ahead, all he said was that he had a new angle on the case. At nine thirty, he walked into a room that was a bit better kept than those in his precinct. "Nice digs. I guess the Feds have a larger budget than the city," Jace quipped.

Before Jace could get settled, Tom fired off his questions. "What have you found out about the Rafkins? Because that car we've been following led us to an old clapboard house on the Long Island beach in Bayville. The funny thing about the owners of that house is they are the same real estate company your old woman purchased her brownstone from back in the early '40s."

"Did you find out who lived in that house and for how long?" Jace asked.

"Sort of. It's an old man who has lived there for more than thirty years and is a well-known bloke who hangs out with his buddies at a pub down the beach. Apparently, he fishes, and has no known source of income other than doing odd jobs for his friends. When he moved out there from the city, he roomed with the previous tenant, an even older guy. That was so long ago that I am guessing he had no job either."

Jace remembered something Sally had said in an off-handed kind of way about her visit to the Gangster Museum. Pulling out his cell phone he looked up the address. "Tom, you aren't going to believe this. There is a museum on the same block as the Rafkin's bookshop. In fact, it's next door. And what a coincidence, the museum has a double entrance... a residence and speakeasy, all connected by underground tunnels. I just had a conversation with an old seaman with Mob history. He said that the buildings on that street all have connecting tunnels. Do you think that the bookshop is part of that community? Could the Rafkins knowingly use those underground tunnels?"

"Are you saying what I think you are? That this old woman is the descendant of one of the Gambino Mob?"

"Tom, this isn't just a murder mystery. This is a trip back to the 1920s. Mob, murder, mayhem," Jace said, and sat back in his chair to absorb what he had just said. Taken aback by the thought of dealing with a Mob family, he wasn't sure how to proceed.

"Jace, I have studied the '30s here in New York, but what could these people have done to make them murder a reporter doing a story on money laundering?"

"I'm thinking if they were dealing in cash, they may have been trading in drugs or sex trafficking. Although, I can't really see that old woman dealing with prostitutes. It has to be more hidden. Extortion would require thugs. I got a glimpse of those two earlier tonight and it's my guess he's educated. Not a thug."

"Forgery?" Tom asked.

"Of what? Have you been alerted to any counterfeit money in circulation? And if not currency, what else? If a young woman hadn't lost her life over this, I'd think this was one of the most interesting puzzles I've ever encountered on the job," Jace said.

"Money laundering in the '20s, '30s, and even the '40s would simply involve opening a foreign bank account," Tom said.

"After the Feds made sure foreign banks reported US citizens' deposits over a certain amount, people could hide income in bearer bonds, which, with today's electronic banking, is no longer easy to do. In the case of drugs, you could use value added cards, you know, like a department store gift card where the origin of the cash isn't disclosed."

"Right, Jace, all outside the banking community and eyes of the US watchdogs."

"Cryptocurrency?" Jace and Tom said simultaneously.

Chapter 33

The next morning, Jace received a call from the mortician. They found a drop of blood under the victim's fingernail and enough Ecstasy to have knocked the victim out for several hours. They sent him the full report and for a moment, he wondered where a search in the police database would lead.

"Drugs to knock out the vic. Now to figure out why? Where was she? How would she have been drugged? Alcohol? Spiked coffee?" Jace said as he thought about the information he'd just received.

Okay, I'll start with the name Rafkin. Working backward, he got a hit on an Aiden, arrested for drunk driving, along with a car full of pals who were out celebrating graduation from Fordham University. The twenty-one-year-old was arrested and booked. The file, dated thirty years ago, showed a younger version of the man he saw with the old woman. This man was a handsome, muscular youth, and the accompanying report had the arrest number, height, weight, address, and contact information. "Bless you, guys, you took a blood sample." Matching it up with the autopsy report, Jace jumped to his feet. The drunken kid's blood type was an exact match. "You bastard. You are going to jail, but first, what else is your family up to? What in hell was the motive for murdering that young woman?"

"Tom, meet me at that diner near your office in fifteen minutes. Urgent," Jace said and, closing his cell phone, grabbed his jacket and headed out the precinct door.

* * *

"What? You're on fire," Tom said before he took a sip of coffee.

"We've got Aiden Rafkin, age fifty-one on murder one." Jace collapsed on his side of the booth. "Now how do we prove motive? This is a Mob family. The grandson isn't going to squeal on Grandma, or his dad, and we don't even know if Daddy is involved. What is the family up to that would require murder?"

Jace sat back and, for the first time since the investigation, felt he would bring Lisa Clark's murderer to justice.

"Jace, I'll check the family out with our crime lab. Maybe we can find something to link the family to that murder, not just the grandson."

"Let me follow up with the apartment building's records and see if we can get a bank account from the Rafkins maintenance check," Jace added. "Another thing, we have to have enough for me to get a search warrant for both Rafkins' apartments, as well as the bookshop. Right now, I only have enough to arrest the grandson for murder. I want to know if that quiet old woman facilitated her grandson's crime."

"If we arrest the two of them at the Rafkin and Sons bookstore, I can gain access to that brownstone and do a thorough search. In order for me to take this up the ladder at the FBI, I will need to find probable cause," Tom explained.

"Well, I can get a search warrant for the bookshop, and you can join my team. But I want to make sure that all the i's are dotted to prevent the charges being thrown out on a technicality. And, just maybe, Tom, my friend in the DA's office, will add warrants for both suspects' apartments."

"How can you be so sure? DAs aren't easy to persuade," Tom asked.

"Because the DA I'm going to visit is a friend of my dad's. And he will understand my need to continue to search for additional information on these two. I want to know what they are up to and if they are Mob connected before I send my men in to arrest Aiden Rafkin," Jace said.

"If my suspicions are right, there is a strong connection with that house on Long Island and the brownstone on St. Mark's Place," Tom said.

"That's your area, friend. I'll continue playing the boyfriend to keep Sally safe and quietly continue digging into those two. But we have to move quickly, Tom. I don't want them spooked."

Chapter 34

The bookshop on St. Mark's Place had been under surveillance for the past week. Now, at 10 a.m., Jace had the police van parked down the street. It was fully equipped to potentially arrest three suspects and have his team conduct a thorough search for evidence surrounding the murder of Lisa Clark. The damaging link to her murder was Aiden Rafkin's DNA found on the skin under the victim's fingernails. With a search warrant in hand, and Tom, having been given official sanction to accompany him on the arrest, Jace was fully prepared to wrap up the case.

"Let's get to it," Jace said as he and a team of seven left the van. Feeling a hand on his shoulder, he looked around. "Jace, I'm just going to follow you, and when you've completed the arrests, Sam and I will continue to search the brownstone."

"Fine."

The early morning sun was strong and reflected in the shop windows, blinding the men from a clear view inside the building. Jace didn't like entering any building without being able to survey the interior. Would he encounter obstacles impeding his movement? Were any of the people inside armed? Clenching his jaw and shoring up mental resolve, he opened the shop door and entered, with the team following close behind.

Spotting his quarry standing behind a counter to his right, he walked over, stood squarely in front, with his eyes never leaving the young man. "I'm Detective Jace Logan," he said, holding up his badge. Seeing the object of his arrest standing quietly, he noticed that Aiden Rafkin did not seem alarmed. "I'm here to arrest you for the murder of Lisa Clark." No reaction. *One cool customer*, he thought, then told him his Miranda rights.

As instructed, the team had walked to various places on the room's perimeter, alert to any new people or problems.

When Aiden looked over Jace's shoulder he turned, and, standing by an open office door, was Mrs. Rafkin, a slim figure in black silk that emphasized the complete loss of color in her face as she observed her grandson's arrest. As she fell to the floor, Jace's team rushed to her aid while he called for a medical team.

"Maronna mia!" Aiden screamed and pushed against Jake, trying to rush to her side. Jace, quick to stop him, twisted him around and handcuffed the frantic man, pushing him to a seated position on the floor.

"Bill?" Jace called across the room, while observing the old woman who lay absolutely still, with one of his team leaning over her and performing CPR. Jace was hoping that she would survive. He wanted to know more about this survivor of a notorious family.

"Heart attack," he replied and quickly moved aside to give access to the medical team that arrived, now rushing to Mrs. Rafkin's side.

Meanwhile, what the announcement of Aiden Rafkin's arrest didn't do, the collapse of his grandmother did, causing him to jump up, buck and twist, all the while muttering Italian curses. Jace knew a few, but most he'd never heard before.

At that moment, a thin rake of a bald-headed man rushed into the room. Pushing aside the medical team, he sank to the floor and cradled Mrs. Rafkin in his arms. "Mr. Rafkin?" Jace called out as he walked to the man's side. The man looked to be in fit condition and, while somewhere in his seventies, moved like someone much younger. Jace had identified him from a photo he'd taken from the bookstore's website. Mrs. Rafkin's son, Alfonso, was the face of Rafkin and Sons, the public persona of this outlet for antiquarian books, but the question remained: what criminal activities were these people involved in that had them to kill Lisa Clark?

Jace reached out to pull Alfonso off the floor and had Bill cuff him. "Let the medics treat your mother." Seeing a look of pure hatred reminded him these were not simply criminals, they were family steeped in an old world of vendettas, murder, and retribution.

"You are under arrest, Mr. Rafkin, along with your son and mother." When Jace stared into the almost-mad eyes, he said a silent prayer.

"What for?" The vehemence in the man's voice echoed in the room.

"For the murder of Lisa Clark," Jace replied. While the man's son, Aiden, had been the actual killer, it was up to the courts to decide what part this man or his mother played in the young reporter's death. Then again, Jace hadn't checked out either Mrs. Rafkin or Aiden's apartments. Once they were booked, he'd take Bill and John for a thorough search.

Jace knew the medical team would treat Mrs. Rafkin and see that she was taken to the hospital where she'd be kept under guard. He was leaving two members of his team behind to search the premises for anything that would indicate the illegal activities.

On the ride to the precinct, Jace wasn't surprised by the stone-faced silence of both Rafkin men. Whatever they were going to do when faced with their arrest for murder, he was almost certain they would let their attorney do all the talking. For some reason, the old gangster movies came to mind, where the lawyer did the talking and was connected to people of influence. Would that keep these people out of jail? he wondered.

I've got my man. Thank God. Now to check out the apartments and see if we can prove how and where the vic was actually killed, Jace thought. *I want to make sure I find enough for the District Attorney to charge everyone involved.*

Chapter 35

Jace, Bill, and John opened the door to Aiden Rafkin's apartment and stood appraising the sparse masculine furnishings. The man was tall and solidly built, so the leather sofa and club chairs were scaled to fit his frame. The sofa long enough for him to stretch out on.

"Bill, why don't you start in the bedroom, and, John, look for all electronic gear. If you find a computer, call me and let's see if the files will be of any value. He might also have a hidden hard drive. In the meantime, I'm going to start with this bookcase," Jace said.

Silence was broken here and there when a door or cabinet drawer was slammed shut. Trying not to destroy the place, Bill and John were experts in pulling everything apart piece at a time, and replacing things as they found them.

After two hours with all electronic equipment, flash drives, and files collected, the three men stood in the middle of the living room and for the first time studied the home of their murderer.

"It is out of a film noir setting," Jace noted. "These carved wood framed furnishings, cut velvet draperies, and a desk of a size to accommodate Aiden Rafkin's huge frame, could have come from Hollywood prop shop."

"My wife would kill me if I ever picked out these heavy drapes with their red and black design," said John. "And the carpet is hardly worn. I don't believe our murderer entertained at home or spent much time here. Everything is in mint condition… just half a century out of date."

"Okay, men, let's see what Grandma's apartment is like," Jace said as he closed down the apartment and the three walked next door.

"Neat as a pin and more tastefully furnished," John said.

"Bill, check out the kitchen. I know how you love to cook and may just find something," Jace directed. "John, check the bedroom, especially pockets, jewelry box, and dresser contents. I'll see if anything looks suspicious here in the living room and dining room."

That's strange, Jace thought as he looked at a ceramic umbrella stand by the front door. There were six umbrellas, five of them with feminine handles and fabrics reminding him of parasols he'd seen in a department store. But the sixth was odd. It was a man's large black umbrella with a curved wood handle. Pulling out a plastic bag, he lifted the umbrella out of the container and wrapped it, hoping that it would have Aiden Rafkin's fingerprints on it.

"John, what do you think of this?" Jace asked when he walked into the room. "You said that the seconds missing from the elevator tape were like a black cloth had been covering the camera. Let's see if this umbrella would do the trick."

Just then, Bill joined the men, holding a bottle of pills. "Look what I just found. Any bets that this is the drug found in the vic's stomach?"

"Guys, over here," John called out after walking to a corner of the room. "Does anyone have a sample bag? This stain looks interesting; I'd like the lab to check it out."

"Drugs, a carpet stain, and possible fingerprints. I'd say we have enough to seal both apartments and have our lab investigate these mysterious items." *Just what I need to take to the DA*, Jace thought.

Chapter 36

Sally had the completed photo albums set out on her dining room table. The album covers were a photo of a dramatic Antarctic landscape of sparkling white- and aqua-tinged snow with a smiling Tyler dressed in the voyage's orange parka with fur-trimmed hood. His smile was pure Tyler showing off and his joy at the magical setting. It was one of the few times he had relinquished the camera so she could capture him and his delight in their romantic adventure.

She had added a title to the photograph so that it looked like a professional magazine cover. *Journey to Antarctica*. It said so much and left out even more.

As she leafed through each double page layout, one depicting scenery, another penguins, and others of the particular animal behaviors that Tyler's patience had captured, it gave her the overview she needed to comprise the letter she would include in each album addressed to each child. Tyler's daughter, Judy, and son, Billy, and Ryan's children, Jane and Mark.

The new graphics program she had purchased for this project enabled her to craft a handwritten note and personalize it for each child. Writing it was the most difficult part of the project. After all, this was where Tyler had died.

Dear [Judy]

Your [dad] [uncle] wanted to bring his excitement about Antarctica and its wildlife back home to you. It was the first time he had witnessed penguins, whales, seals, and birds in their natural habitat going about their lives, taking care of their young, feeding, and just relaxing in the sun. Each photo lovingly captures the wonders he so enjoyed and is now sharing with you.

His camera contains over four hundred photos, and I have included some of the best in this album.

With all his love, and mine.

Sally

With a deep sigh, after inserting the personalized letter in the beginning of each album, Sally sat back, trying to recapture what was too short a time, but one she now considered a wonderful gift.

The ringing of her phone brought her back to reality. "Yes?" Hearing Jace's excited voice made her wonder what was expected of her next.

"Sally, it's over. Can I stop by and answer all those questions I was unable to before?"

"Over? Like you caught the murderer?"

"Yes. Can I stop by?" She didn't know how to answer. This was mid-November, two and a half months since she stepped out of her apartment and onto a merry-go-round of murder and mystery.

"Really over?" She didn't know how she felt, but didn't want to hear about it alone. "Jace, could you stop by tomorrow at noon? I'd like Ryan, Jeanne, and my mom to hear what you have to say. They have tried not to show their concern, but I know they want to know as badly as I do who and why that nice young woman was killed."

"Yes, Sally. I understand. Till noon tomorrow. Bye."

The news should have been comforting. But thinking back to the fateful August morning, she realized that for the previous three years, she had been on automatic. The investigation had slowly brought her back to life. Being in the midst of a murder investigation had been like a splinter you couldn't remove…an annoyance always there to take you away from your real life.

Dialing her mother's number, Sally was trying to think of just what to say. "Mom, could you come into the city tomorrow morning?" Sally asked in as calm a voice as possible. Her nerves had just settled in her stomach and the phone was sticking in her sweaty hand.

"Of course, dear. Can you tell me what this is all about?" Barbara asked.

"Oh, I think they've solved the murder and Detective Logan is stopping by to fill me in." Sally wasn't sure, but she thought her mom had taken a deep breath. "How about ten? I'll have coffee and freshly baked muffins," Sally added, hoping the simple offering of food would make the meeting seem less traumatic.

"Of course." Just hearing her mother's calm but upbeat reply was a relief. Barbara hadn't said much about the investigation, but Sally read all the tension in her voice every time they talked. Now it was over.

Now to Jeanne and Ryan. The phone had only rung once when Jeanne answered. "Hi, Jeanne. Are you and Ryan free tomorrow around eleven? If so, could you stop by?"

"You're engaged," Jeanne replied in her usual teasing way.

"Maybe instead of working with patients at the hospital, you should be running a matchmaking service for doctors and nurses too busy to have a personal life." Laughing with her best friend did what Jace's news hadn't; it made Sally relax. "Anyway, Detective Logan is coming by at noon to tell me about solving the murder. It's over."

"We'll be there earlier. Thank you for including us. We've been worried sick about this whole thing."

"Tomorrow, around eleven. And thanks."

Chapter 37

Barbara arrived at ten and, looking at the coffee table set up with nibbles of fruit and nuts, smiled. "Sally, I can't wait to meet this detective. And to find out the end of the mystery."

"Here, Mom, coffee. Muffins in the kitchen."

"A celebration to the end of the mystery. I like that."

Ryan and Jeanne arrived next. "Champagne, for a celebration. One mystery solved, and my favorite sister-in-law's freedom."

Promptly at noon, her doorman rang to announce Jace. "Please send him up," she replied and, hanging up the phone, turned to the group settled around the coffee table.

As soon as she opened the door, Jace grabbed her in a huge hug. Taken aback, all Sally could do was stare. Who was this man? Not the careful, polite, official she'd been seeing all this time.

Stepping aside, she led Jace to the living room, where Ryan stood, and walking over to Jace, shook his hand. With a slap to his shoulder, he turned. "Detective Jace Logan, this is my wife Jeanne, and Sally's mom, Barbara Compton."

Stunned by Ryan's behavior, Sally suddenly got it. Ryan liked and approved of this man.

"Jace, why don't you take the club chair and tell us what this has all been about," Sally said, reclaiming her role as hostess. There was nothing in anyone's reaction, including Jace, that seemed awkward. They had accepted him into their group. *Thank you, Ryan, for breaking the ice.*

"Let me start at the beginning. Sally reported something she had seen on the floor of an elevator to the doorman, who checked it on the building security camera and, finding that it was a person, locked the elevator, brought it to the sub-basement and called the police. When the officers saw the murdered woman, they called the precinct, and since I was on duty, it became my case."

Sally saw her mother begin to ask a question, and Jace, holding up his hand to stop her. With a smile, he continued. "We normally interview everyone in the building to see if we can gather information about the victim. Or if they had ever seen her. Then we look into the victim's background, and her home for additional clues. But in this instance, there was no identification on the body." Jace then looked over at Sally. "And if it hadn't been for Sally recognizing the fabric of her coat and mentioning that it looked like something in her client's store, it could have taken us far longer to identify the young woman, Lisa Clark."

She was embarrassed. While she had already told this to the others, this attention was unfamiliar. She never expected to be praised for being observant.

"So why was she murdered?" Jeanne asked, never one to wait.

"She had been investigating a family business that she believed to be behind a large money laundering scheme." Jace had to hold up his hand again, this time because Ryan was about to ask a question.

"Money laundering may have been her focus, but we found that this family has roots going back to the Italian Mob of the '20s."

"Money laundering in the '20s?" Sally asked. "From what I've learned, they just put it in a safe."

"Yes. We haven't found it yet. But we did connect Aiden Rafkin to Lisa Clark's murder. Apparently, when he was strangling her, she scratched his neck and his blood was found under one of her nails."

"So…" Jeanne began.

"So, Mrs. Scott, once we identified him, we began to look into the family and its business. I don't want to frighten you, but Sally was followed when she visited the precinct. We brought in the FBI and they followed the man who had followed her. That led to a smuggling ring run out of Bayville, Long Island."

"What has that to do with money laundering?" Barbara asked.

"Let me recap. The young woman was writing an exposé. She thought it was about one thing, but once we connected Lisa to the Rafkins, it became more complicated. Apparently,

Mrs. Rafkin is the daughter of a confederate of Joe Gambino, head of one of the five Italian Mob families in New York. He ran the family business until he was sent to jail. And at seventeen she became her father's heir apparent continuing his business of extortion and sex trafficking. After her son was born, she purchased a brownstone on St. Mark's place and opened an antiquarian bookshop. Not wanting to continue running her dad's operation, she focused on forgery of legal documents."

"But…" Sally began, only pausing when Jace once again held up his hand to stop her.

"World War II gave Mrs. Rafkin a new focus. With war brewing, she expanded into expert replication of official documents needed by those who wanted to sneak into this country. We found evidence of expertly forged passports, driver's licenses, and other proof of someone's identity at the time of our arrests."

"That old woman ran a Mob?" Sally asked. "She's fragile. Old. And who is that man she is never without?"

"Ah, her grandson, Aiden, who is a Fordham University graduate with an MBA in finance. He runs her books."

"But how did you connect Mrs. Rafkin to the actual murder?" Sally asked, details getting her confused.

"On watching the building videotapes from the security cameras, we followed Ms. Clark from the time she visited her aunt on the fifth floor, and again when she left her aunt's apartment. But she didn't leave the building. Instead, she took the elevator to the fifteenth floor. We didn't know who she was seeing, but the next time she was spotted was the following day, lying dead on the elevator floor."

Jace turned to Sally and saw that she hadn't yet put the pieces together. "Due to the lack of bodily fluids in the elevator, we knew Lisa had been murdered someplace else. When we searched Mrs. Rafkin's apartment, we found pills of Ecstasy, like the drug the autopsy found in Lisa, in a bottle in Mrs. Rafkin's kitchen. In addition to the drugs, we found some of Lisa's DNA on Mrs. Rafkin's living room carpet… Even though it was a tiny spot on the edge of her carpet hidden under her sofa, it was enough to prove that the murder had taken place there."

"But how did Lisa's body get into the elevator without anyone seeing it?" Jeanne asked.

"Ah, very astute, Mrs. Scott. We also found a man's umbrella in Mrs. Rafkin's umbrella stand. When we opened it at the entrance of the elevator, it totally blacked out the camera. Fingerprints on the handle were of the Rafkin's driver with a police record of his own."

"So now that you have the murderer, what about money laundering, the supposed focus of that unfortunate reporter's research?" Barbara said.

"Mrs. Scott, do you ever watch those 1940s films of the Italian Mob? Well, they do not, under any circumstance, turn on one of their own. And this is blood, with the grandmother, her son, who we believe is an expert forger, and grandson who handles the family's finances. We aren't sure we will be able to connect them to money laundering. All we have proved is that Aiden Rafkin killed Lisa Clark. The DA will have to prove that Mrs. Rafkin and her son were accomplices."

"But the smuggling? Their bank accounts? Can you get to those?" Ryan interrupted.

Jace shook his head no. "Ryan, tying up that business is now in the hands of the FBI. I have solved my case, uncovered the motive, and caught the murderer and possibly his accomplices. What is important is they are in jail awaiting trial." Looking over at Sally, he added, "And Sally is safe."

"And the FBI? Where does Sally fit in with them?" Ryan asked.

"Ryan. I promise you, Sally is no longer a connection to their end of things. The FBI has begun investigating the Rafkins' wider operation. What were they smuggling into the country? How were they paid? Unless there is another branch of the family, or employees who can continue to implement this scheme, it's over."

Sally sat quietly, trying to absorb the complexity of the Rafkin's operation. The fact that their ties went back to the days of Joe Gambino chilled her. She lived in a building of normal people. Certainly not criminals, or the head of a clan of gangsters.

"Sally," Barbara asked. "Are you alright? I thought you would be happy that this is over."

As she looked at her mom, she realized just how worried everyone had been about her. "Thank you all for being there for me. I'll be fine." Turning to look at Jace, she realized she owed him an answer as well. "Jace, I guess I'm stunned that after all this time, living in fear, I can get back to my life."

"Okay," Ryan said and, lifting Sally from her chair, gave her a hug and kiss on the cheek. Jeanne rushed over and enveloped her in a tight hug, whispering, "Call me."

Sally nodded as her mother opened the door for them to leave and noticed that Ryan bent down to say something and watched Barbara reach up and kiss his cheek.

"Mrs. Compton, it was a pleasure to meet you. I have to leave, but I know Sally is in good hands," Jace said and took the hand Barbara offered. He didn't so much as shake it as give it a warm squeeze. With another look at the unusually quiet Sally, he wished they were alone. This reaction was akin to shock. "Okay then. I'll show myself out."

When the door closed, Barbara reached out and pulled her daughter into her arms. Sally's head dropped to her shoulder, and she began to cry. The apartment was quiet. "Honey, it will take time."

Chapter 38

Sleep just wouldn't come. After tangling up in her sheets, Sally got up and headed for the kitchen. A cup of tea might soothe her jangled nerves.

Settled with a steaming cup and stretching out on the living room sofa, she closed her eyes. The past few months flew past in her mind and each time the picture stopped, she saw Jace. She must have dozed off because when she opened her eyes, dawn was just breaking and her mom was entering the living room.

"Have you been here all night?" Barbara asked. "Well, I don't know about you, but a strong cup of coffee and some of those muffins you baked are just what I need. Why not join me in the kitchen?" she said.

"Okay. Give me a minute and I'll wash my face," Sally said and left her mother, not ready to hear any advice on something she couldn't get a grip on herself.

"Here, I heated the muffins and pulled out the butter and jam. I'm glad you haven't forgotten how to make apricot butter. It's my favorite."

"Uh huh."

"Let's eat." Barbara's cheerful voice cleared away some of Sally's mental fog.

"Mom, I'm sorry for breaking down last night," Sally said, settling at the place Barbara had set up for her. "I don't really know what to think about the whole thing."

"Why not try putting those thoughts into words? I'm a good listener," Barbara said and took a sip of her coffee. "That detective seems nice."

"Uh huh," Sally replied.

"Ryan seems to like him."

"Mom, I'm sorry. I just don't know anything anymore. It's taken me three years to finally finish furnishing this apartment, making it a home. And to build a business with clients I enjoy working with. I'm paying my way. And Jace?" Sally took a large sip of coffee. "Ouch. It's hot."

Barbara smiled. "Yes. You have come a long way. I especially love the way you have included me into your family. Jeanne and Ryan, and all the kids. Grandchildren I never thought to have."

"Yes. Family. All I've ever wanted with Tyler."

"And now?"

"Well, back in August, I was settled and living my new life when I became involved in this murder investigation. And the drama, fear, and looking to see if I was being followed. Now that it's all over, I feel hollow. Empty." As she looked to her mother for some answer, she saw not concern, but a soft smile. "Mom?"

"Tell me, how often did you see this detective?"

"Oh, maybe a couple of times a week in the beginning. Then he took me to dinner a few times."

"What did you talk about? The murdered woman?"

"That's the strange part. Jace couldn't talk about the case, but every time we met, he'd ask questions. About the building staff, or the residents, or some other detail relating to this building. And sometimes, he'd leave saying that I'd said something he needed to check out."

"So, for almost three months, you have spent quite a bit of time with this nice young man. What's he like? The man I just met seemed genuinely concerned about you."

"Concerned. Now that I think about it, Jace made me feel safe. He was interested in what I was doing, my opinion on things. Unlike Tyler, where I took care of him." She stopped her coffee cup halfway to her mouth and looked at her mom. "He made me feel I was the most important person in this entire mess. Why haven't I realized that?"

"Maybe because being in his company felt natural? He didn't want anything, and was always there to support you?"

Sally, thinking about what her mom had said, realized Jace had been a calm and reassuring presence during the past months.

"Look, kiddo. I'm going to take an early train home. Why not take a long hot bath and give that nice young man a call? I think he should at the very least know you appreciate his kind attention to you all these months."

Chapter 39

By the time Sally had relaxed in a hot bath and dressed, she was calm enough to consider her mother's advice. But what could she say to Jace? It didn't take long before she recognized her true feelings. The reason for her pretending all these months that Jace wasn't more than the detective in charge of the murder investigation. *You're right, Mom, I owe him a call.*

Reaching for her address book, she picked up the card Jace had given her when they first met and, turning it over, saw his private number. "It's now or never, old girl."

"Happy Sunday, Jace. Am I calling you at a bad time?" Sally began, not even waiting for Jace to speak.

"No. Of course not."

"I wanted to apologize for not being more enthusiastic yesterday. You know… that the case is solved and I'm finally safe."

"I guess you were stunned. You know, learning that it was finally over."

"Well, yes, sort of. Jace, would it be possible for us to meet someplace and just let me talk about it all?" Sally didn't really know what else to say and hoped that in person she'd finally have the words to express her confusion. Could she, would she let herself feel for this kind man? Jace had a way that usually encouraged her to say things before she had thoroughly thought them through. When she was with him, her natural censors seemed to fall away.

"Now that the case is over, we can meet and talk anytime, anywhere you want." His voice quietly expressed his thoughts.

"It's not exactly about the case or the past three months. Just something I feel I have to say. You have been nothing but patient with me… my confusion about me, my life."

"Sally, you just gave me an idea. Can you take Monday off? Not the whole day, just the morning. I'd like to take a drive up to the mountains later today and show you my family cabin. We could stay overnight and come back first thing Monday. It's a three-hour drive, so we can leave at noon and be back on Monday morning."

"Ah…" She didn't know what to think. Overnight? Alone with this person she couldn't stop thinking about?

Hearing her hesitation, Jace asked quietly, "Don't you think you can trust me by now?"

"Yes. And yes, I'd love to take a trip away from the city. Anyway, you've never really told me much about your life. I'd like to see the private Jace Logan."

"That's the Sally I know. I'll pick you up at noon," Jace said, and he hung up before she could reply.

Chapter 40

The drive and soothing music enabled Sally to postpone thoughts of what she was going to say to Jace… about her feelings… for him, the investigation, her future hopes. The easy conversation was all about the country life he had lived as a child.

"So here we are. The cabin that my brothers and I helped my dad to build all those years ago," Jace said with a lightness and joy she hadn't seen before.

It was a two-story wood home that blended in with the countryside. Not some modern painted wood design that, while neat and functional, was devoid of personality. The front porch looked out to the mountains of upstate New York, with not a telephone pole or strip mall in sight. The leaves were tinged with the changes of autumn, and a more colorful and peaceful sight Sally had never seen. Her home with Tyler was in a built-up suburban area where houses were on plots, not in settings dressed in Mother Nature's finest.

"Oh, how beautiful," Sally said, a smile wreathing her face and her voice filled with wonder.

"I just knew you would appreciate my secret home away from the city," Jace said and, hopping out, walked around to help Sally from the car. As he reached into the back seat for her overnight bag, his shoulder brushed hers and, turning with his face inches away from hers, leaned down and gave her a light kiss.

For Sally, all sounds stopped. Her stomach was aflutter. *So this is what I've been missing all these years*, she thought. Tyler was all crazy with sexual heat. Here was a man whose light kiss was a promise of a different kind of passion. Slow to build and sensitive to her feelings.

The mood was broken when Jace moved aside to let her step from the car. Hand in hand they walked to the entrance and with key in lock, Jace opened the door and stepped aside to let Sally enter.

Still feeling the effects of his kiss, Sally stood inside the entrance of a large main room furnished in an upholstered sofa and chairs. The room's centerpiece was a river stone wall and built-in fireplace large enough to keep logs burning for hours.

"Oh, Jace, this is magical," she gushed.

"I'd hoped you would like my hideaway. It reminds me why I do my job, so people can live safely in peace."

Sally began to walk around the room, noticing little things that spelled male. "I guess you and your brothers didn't bring girlfriends, wives, or kids here," she said, more as a question.

"No. Actually, this was a family home with my brothers and our friends joining my parents on weekends. It was like a camp with hiking, swimming and in winter skiing."

"And now?"

"Well, my brother Andy was killed in Afghanistan a few years ago. My older brother Liam moved with his wife and my two nephews to Florida years ago, where he is a captain in the local fire department."

"And your parents? Didn't you tell me they passed away while you were overseas with the Marines?"

"My mom died of cancer while I was in high school, so my dad raised us on his own. He was a New York City policeman and died while I was overseas. Maybe because we idolized my dad, we all continued in his tradition of service," Jace said, more as an afterthought.

While Jace disappeared with their bags, Sally spotted the American Flag given to the family of fallen military sons and daughters. Next to it was a small frame with a Silver Star commemorating Andrew Logan's service.

"Ah, you've seen Andy's medal," Jace said as he walked to her side. "Look, Sally, I've placed your bag in the bedroom to the right of the kitchen; my room is upstairs."

She knew he would be the perfect gentleman, but was that what she wanted?

* * *

Sally, accustomed to being the host of any party, was surprised by the efficient preparations for dinner. Jace had opened a bottle of wine and as they both sipped, he skillfully chopped onions, peppers, crushed garlic, and began preparing what she guessed would be a rich tomato sauce. All the while, he told her bits of family happenings at the cabin. It all sounded so idyllic. Especially since Sally was an only child.

"Jace, you are so good at this. Do you cook often?" she asked.

Laughing, he took a sip of wine and winked. "How do you think I've lived all these years as a bachelor? I'm good at grilling steak, can make my mom's recipe for spaghetti sauce, and occasionally read a recipe."

"I am impressed."

"Let's take our wine to the living room and let the sauce simmer awhile," Jace suggested as he placed his hand on her back and headed to the next room.

Settled on the sofa, Sally turned to face Jace, then looking away, decided it was now or never and placed her wineglass on the coffee table. "Jace, I'm grateful for your kindness, thoughtfulness, and protection. This entire murder investigation that kept putting us together made me take a good look at my life. You know most of it. I was married to a man I deeply loved, and he died in an accident. What you probably didn't realize, something I have only gotten a grasp of myself, but I've managed to close off everything in life and focus solely on building a new home and livelihood. As my mother and Jeanne keep reminding me, I wasn't living. I was frozen in the past."

Jace placed his hands on either side of her face and raised her head to look into his eyes. "Sally, when we talk about personal things, I would like us to see one another."

Nodding yes, she felt him remove his hands and at first looked down at her own, clenched, then with a small smile looked up. Just as she was going to continue, the kitchen timer rang, and Jace patted her hands, jumped up, and walked into the kitchen. On his return, with a wink and a smile, he refreshed her glass and resettled on the couch, a bit closer than before.

"Ah," she began.

"You were saying before we were interrupted?"

"Your sauce?"

"Oh, I turned it off. It will only take maybe another fifteen minutes to finish."

Nodding, Sally looked into his eyes and, seeing nothing but warmth, decided to just blurt it out. "Well, Jace, I don't easily trust people. A bad habit, but one you have found a way around. Maybe it was that poor girl's death, but probably because of the time you took to make sure I was safe... whatever it was... is, my feelings have grown beyond trust. So..."

Sally didn't finish her confession of love. Jace had pulled her into his arms and, with a long, hot yet tender kiss, ended that topic, permanently. Sally was in love. It was as if her body had become fused to his. More than a sexual passion, this was a complete heart and soul experience, one she no longer wanted to fight.

Breaking away, Jace once again held her face, gently stroking her cheeks with his thumbs. "You don't need words, Sally. I'd fallen in love with you months ago and knew you weren't ready to let go of the past."

"Jace…" she began.

"Let me finish. I don't believe you really know yourself. Yes, you are fully in control of your skills and home. But in my line of work, it is rare to find someone clueless about how they are seen by others. And you, my love, have an open heart to see and hear others' pain and joy. From the little bit Ryan shared, even with the tragic death of your husband, you live life in a straightforward manner, rejecting any negativity many in this city seem to attract." Jace couldn't continue. He needed to hear what she would say.

Sally had listened and heard what Jace was saying, but didn't know how to respond.

"Sally?"

Smiling, she reached up and drew Jace into a deep kiss. "Yes, I see now. And, with a clear mind am offering my love."

It was a beginning. But Sally was going to give her all to this man and just maybe in return she'd find herself… her own hopes and dreams, and above all, her need to be loved.

The End

What She Didn't Know – Book 3

Grasping life with both hands

"It's never too late to be what you might have been."

~ George Eliot

Sally Compton Scott has finally broken free of her tightly controlled life as a widow and opened herself to new challenges.

Her accounting business is humming along, she's in love, and her unbridled curiosity draws her to a new project, finishing the explosive book that Lisa Clark, the murdered young reporter, never got to write.

Were the criminals, now in custody, guilty of more than the reporter's murder? Has this secretive family's business been closed down for good? Are their crimes about money laundering, or something more sinister?

Sally's life is brimming with romance, mystery, and new challenges. What she hadn't counted on was once again placing herself in danger.

* * *

Sally Scott was about to pick up a book and escape reality by immersing herself into the fictional life of an adventurous woman, far braver than herself. It was just the remedy after a busy day preparing her clients' taxes. This mystery was the latest in a series about a lone woman, Catey Brown, traveling the country, shunning all thoughts of permanence in either a home or social relationships.

Settled in her favorite club chair with a cup of tea, Sally couldn't wait to see what trouble Catey would get into and out of next. Just the character's background provided Sally with adventures and problems she knew she would never have in her own rather conventional life.

Catey Brown wanted to experience all kinds of adventures that staying at home and getting some job wouldn't have provided. At eighteen she took to the road, earning her way in various jobs that weren't too fussy about credentials. Sometimes she stopped in one place long enough to take a course in a topic of interest. Topics like law enforcement, robbery, or crimes of passion that were often taught at local colleges.

Deep into the early pages of her book, Sally was surprised by the ringing of her doorbell. One of the things she loved about living in a New York City high-rise was that people called ahead, they didn't just drop in unannounced. Opening her door, she saw her neighbor. "Mrs. Clark, this is a pleasant surprise," she said with a welcoming smile for the older woman.

"Sally, hi. I know this is sudden, but I wondered if you had a little time. There is something that is niggling at me, and you might just be able to help."

It wasn't so much the idea of welcoming her, of course she would. She liked the woman and felt sorry about the death of her niece. But Sally saw the forced smile hid something more serious than a neighborly visit. Living in a building of some 200 apartments, neighbors knew one another by sight, but even when they shared chit chat and a bit on topics of the day, you couldn't really call them friends. As for Mrs. Clark, they were a bit closer, having spoken over the past several months in connection with the murder of her niece, an up-and-coming reporter. Sally was the one who spotted something amiss in their building's elevator that turned out to be Lisa Clark's body. An experience that thrust Sally into the midst of a full-scale murder investigation lasting several months.

After Sally settled Mrs. Clark in the living room, she sat in a nearby chair. "How may I be of help?"

"Actually, I was wondering if you might be interested in an idea I had. I was going through Lisa's things, now that the police have released the apartment back to me, and found a couple of notebooks. In each, the beginning third were simply family recipes. But as I flipped through the pages, I found notes on that book about money laundering she was working on."

Sally caught her breath. The police hadn't found anything that uncovered the money laundering activities Lisa was investigating. Even though Lisa's death had been avenged with the arrest of her murderer, it didn't deal with Lisa's obsession with writing an explosive exposé on the Rafkin family. Her tenacity in following leads to solve still unproven crimes had led to her murder.

"And you were thinking of finishing the book for Lisa?" Sally asked in awe of the woman's plan. As far as she knew, when the murderer and associates, all named Rafkin, were arrested, nothing was discovered to account for an additional crime of money laundering. The mother, son, and grandson were arrested in connection with Lisa's murder, and the additional crime of forgery.

"You see, these notes showed that the family, while they go back to the 20's Italian Mafia, the Rafkins, were actually involved in a very modern series of activities."

"You've got my attention," Sally said, holding her breath. She had often thought that if she hadn't seen the cloth on the floor of the elevator before the doors closed in her face, or hadn't reported it to the doorman so quickly, the person involved in the woman's death would have had time to remove the body and no one would have been the wiser.

"You know, Mrs. Clark, I have always felt somewhat connected to the police investigation into your niece's death. If you are truly going to finish her project, I would love to help."

"Then you must stop being so formal and call me Susan."

"Agreed. Now that the formalities are over," Sally said with a smile. "How about a cup of tea?"

With tea and cookies set before them on the kitchen table, Susan relaxed. "I have never written a book. I retired several years ago from a book publishing company, working as a senior assistant to one of its executives," Susan began and, taking a sip of tea, looked at Sally to see if she seemed interested.

"Nor am I familiar with police tactics or procedures. Balancing my bank account is the scope of my mathematical capabilities," she said, pausing as if waiting for Sally to respond. "So, maybe we could complete Lisa's research, and you might complete the book? There I've said it!"

"Phew. Write a book, Susan? The money aspect of any research would be fun and certainly in my skill set," Sally mused. "But a book? One that would do your niece justice?"

"Couldn't we take it one step at a time? Research what the Rafkins were really up to. Where they have hidden their ill-gotten gains, large enough they would require money being laundered? In today's world where the government knows everything, how would they have done it?"

"Yes. I don't think the police have figured that one out. But, Susan, on a personal note, remember that nice detective, Jace Logan? Well, I've been seeing him… So, maybe I could talk to him and see what they uncovered when they made their arrests?" Sally said.

"I've seen you two together and hoped it was more personal than solving Lisa's murder. You just look so right together," Susan added. "And I can promise you I certainly won't say anything."

Author's Note

Each book begins with finding a female characteristic that fascinates me and is somewhat removed from my personal journey. That characteristic is usually some weakness in the way a woman sees herself and reacts to her circumstances.

As a novelist, my next search is for some crisis that will force my protagonist to go beyond her comfort zone, and fight to resolve the problem before it consumes her.

"Now that you, the reader, have spent time in the worlds I have created, I welcome your thoughts. They provide guidance for those stories yet to be told.

For those of you who have enjoyed *What She Didn't Know - Book 2 - Of Widowhood and Murder*, I ask you to write a review and post it on Amazon for others to find.

Thank you in advance.

Patricia E. Gitt

What She Didn't Know- Book 1

Blinded by love

Sally Compton Scott felt blessed with her marriage to the magnetic Tyler Scott. He was her everything. A successful executive at a marketing company, a passionate lover and considerate partner.

She was looking forward to starting their family. Children she could love, cuddle, and raise to interesting adults.

Her life was perfect. Until it wasn't.

"OMG what an amazing book. I literally could not put this book down. I stayed up all night till 6am to finish it then went to sleep and alarm went off at 9.45am! shattered but loved it so much. Great characters ☆ ☆ ☆ ☆"

"The perfect weekend read! I was not expecting this book to be so dang good!

Literally I was hooked reading the blurb. This was a very quick read for me! I couldn't put my Kindle down long enough to do anything. The only thing I didn't care much for was the pacing I felt started off slow! But other than that a really good quick book! ☆ ☆ ☆ ☆"

https://www.amazon.com/What-She-Didnt-Know-fairytale-ebook/dp/B093JYTJMZ